LITTLE WHITE LIE

by

Lea Santos

2010

ISBN 10: 1-60282-163-1
ISBN 13: 978-1-60282-163-7

This Trade Paperback Original Is Published By
Bold Strokes Books, Inc.
P.O. Box 249
Valley Falls, NY 12185

First Edition: July 2010

CREDITS
Editor: Stacia Seaman
Production Design: Stacia Seaman
Cover Design By Sheri (graphicartist2020@hotmail.com)

Acknowledgments

Big ups to the stellar staff at BSB: Len Barot, Shelley Thrasher, Cindy Cresap, LD Anderson, Connie Ward, Stacia Seaman, Sheri, Paula Tighe, Ruth Sternglantz (I don't know that you worked on the book, Ruth, but you're just cool), and all the rest of you. Also props to my long-suffering family (I know, I know—there should be a registry for workaholic psychos like me), to the oft-ignored friends who stood by when I was verging on apoplectic with a ten-layer cake of deadline and—mostly—life stress…in particular Rachel, Nell and Trin, Georgia, Heather, the other Heather, Terri Clark, Deb Jones Parker, the Bad Girls (you know who you are) and the ever-pink and awesome Horatio. My yogi guides, Tara, Jennifer, Dakini, Ruthann, Maya, Nancy, and Sasha for the much-needed sanity breaks. And the biggest, most heartfelt thanks to… well…to coffee. Sorry, dudes, it is what it is.

Dedication

For LaRita

CHAPTER ONE

Emie Jaramillo wiped her damp palms down the side seams of her slacks and wondered, briefly, if the taupe suit her friends had insisted she wear had been the proper choice for her first—and probably only—television appearance. They'd fussed through a mountain of clothes in her hotel room that morning while she sat in the corner and reviewed her notes, amused by their fashion-plate antics. She supposed the tailored silk ensemble they'd settled on projected a conservative enough image to offset her controversial topic: human cloning.

Now, if only she could be cloned from the gracious and brilliantly spoken Maya Angelou for this talk-show stint, life would be just peachy. Speaking to the science community was stressful enough. But trying to explain the truth about cloning to the general public, rife with all the misconceptions and misplaced fears? Sometimes, she wondered what she'd been thinking, accepting this gig. A smirk lifted one corner of her mouth as she glanced around the cramped makeup studio located backstage of the set of *The Barry Stillman Show*.

Four beige walls, adorned with framed photos of previous guests, surrounded the beauty parlor chair she occupied. A filing cabinet claimed one corner, with an iPod docking station perched atop it. Rolling metal racks behind her held a mishmash of garments, perhaps for guests who had fashion emergencies before they were due onstage. Along with the rescue clothes hung a few smocks smeared with makeup streaks. Before her stood a long countertop stacked with more pots and jars and bottles of cosmetics than she'd ever seen, and above the counter hung a huge mirror that framed the reflection of her, as usual, un-made-up face.

The hot bulbs circling the mirror glared off the lenses of her wire-framed eyeglasses and melted the creamy cosmetics piled before her. If the makeup lights were hot, Emie could only imagine what it would feel like beneath the strong stage lights in front of All Those People. She shuddered, fending off another tsunami of nerves. At least her parents and her best friends, Iris and Paloma, would be out there for moral support. She reminded herself to look for their smiling faces in the audience the minute she got out onstage.

Speaking of faces—Emie pushed her glasses atop her head and leaned forward to squint at her own mug. Ugh.

Bland. Boring, she supposed. Such superficialities hadn't bothered her for decades, but after a lighting test, the camera operator had informed the production manager that she looked "pale as a corpse." Swell. Just what she needed to hear to calm her nerves.

Emie was the first to concede she'd landed on the plain side of the looks spectrum, but so what? She liked herself just fine. Now, her hair—she turned her head from side to side and arranged the short wisps as best she could with a few plucks and twists of her fingers. The close-cropped style looked great on Halle Berry. Not quite the same effect on her. She sat back in the chair, until her reflection was nothing but a myopic blur. All this microscopic focus on her *looks* left her feeling…squirmy. She wasn't used to it. No one expected female scientists to be bombshells, anyway, and although that stereotype had always rankled purely on principle, deep down Emie couldn't care less. Still, she was grateful a professional would be applying her makeup for the show, if only to evict the "pale as a corpse" proclamation and ease some of her nervousness. She'd release herself to the process, just for today. A woman could be vain once in her life, couldn't she?

She glanced at her watch and wondered where the miracle-working makeup person might be. The producer had stuck her head in the room earlier and told Emie she'd go on in fifteen minutes. That didn't leave them much time to breathe some life back into her complexion.

As if on cue, the door opened, and in walked— Emie plunked her glasses back on the bridge of her nose and turned. Her breath caught. What the hell? Her breath *never* caught. But, Lord, this woman was sex personified, and even Emie couldn't deny it. Broad-shouldered and bronze-skinned, she wore faded, form-fitting Levi's, low-heeled black boots, and a tight black T-shirt emblazoned with *The Barry Stillman Show* in red lettering. And if Emie's mama only knew what images the woman's shiny black ponytail brought to her mind, there'd be a chorus of Hail Marys uttered in her soul's defense within minutes.

"Dr. Jaramillo?"

"Yes?" Her hand fluttered to her throat, an involuntary reaction she nevertheless regretted immediately.

"I'm Gia Mendez, your makeup artist," she said, her husky voice smooth as crème de menthe. "You're the brilliant scientist I've been hearing so much about, yes?" She flashed Emie a movie-star smile and extended a long-fingered hand for a handshake.

Emie nodded slowly, ignoring the heated flush she felt creeping up her neck at Gia's compliment. Disconcerted, she glanced from her face to her hand, then back at her face before she did her part to complete the handshake.

"Dios mío," she whispered more than spoke as the makeup artist's warm palm slid against hers. If women like Gia Mendez were commonplace in Chicago, she'd clone the whole darn city and become the hero of the lesbian population. All hail the

miracle-working corpse. The thought curved her mouth into a private smile.

Gia released her hand and asked, "Nervous?" She turned her back to switch on the purple iPod, filling the room with hot Mary J. Blige tunes, then began assembling brushes and pencils and pots of color, her focus on the tools of her trade.

"A-a little," Emie admitted, content just to watch Gia move about the close quarters they shared. Her movements were skilled and confident. Gia fell squarely on the androgynous side, but her graceful movements added an intriguing layer. This was probably Emie's one chance in life to have a woman like Gia Mendez lay hands on her, and she'd be a damned liar if she claimed she wasn't thrilled by the prospect. "Okay, a lot."

"It always seems to hit people once I come in to do their makeup." Gia winked.

Emie's heart plunged before snapping back up to lodge in her throat. That wink should be classified as a lethal weapon.

"You have my sympathy," Gia continued, seemingly oblivious to Emie's knocked-mute admiration. "I much prefer remaining behind the scenes."

Emie pulled herself out of the irritating lust-induced stupor and cleared her throat. "I'm a behind-the-scenes woman myself, although I've, ah, never been on television before." *She probably knows that, silly*, Emie chastised herself. This focused sexy female attention was rattling her composure. She wasn't used to it. "It's not too often a scientist has such an opportunity. I'm very flattered." She nudged her glasses up with the knuckle of her pointer finger. "My parents and friends are in the audience." She cast her gaze down briefly, not wanting to appear too prideful.

Gia peered at her, her expression darkening for an instant before she turned away. Emie wondered if she'd said something wrong, but the moment quickly passed so she dismissed it.

"Tell me about your research, Emie—may I call you that?"

"Of course."

Gia faced her, crossed toned arms over her chest, then

leaned back against the counter, a position that accentuated the sculpted muscles in her upper body. The bright lights shadowed the curves of her cheekbones and glinted off the single diamond stud in Gia's earlobe. Emie forced her mind from its idiotic awe of this woman and back onto her question.

"Research? Research. Yes. Human cloning, that's what I research." She laughed lightly, shaking her head. "And, well, it's a touchy subject."

"How so?"

"Oh, you know. Lots of moral and religious implications. My grandmother prays daily for my soul. She thinks my colleagues and I are trying to play God. If I ever actually clone a human being, I'll probably be excommunicated from the church. Not that I would clone a human being, but…well, I guess that's what I'm here to do. Dispel the myths." Emie ran her fingers through her hair and shrugged one shoulder.

Gia chuckled, holding several different colored lipsticks next to Emie's cheek. "Your grandmother sounds a lot like mine. Let me guess. Catholic?"

"But of course," Emie told her, tone wry. "So I continue to do the research, but I feel guilty about it."

Gia leaned her head back and laughed, giving Emie an excellent view of her long dancer's neck, her straight white teeth. *Talk, Emie. Stay on track.*

"We're not necessarily trying to create people, though," she blurted, averting her gaze from the seductive hollow at Gia's throat. "And forgive me if I'm telling you facts you already know. But there are plenty of other medically plausible reasons to clone human cells. It's still a little too sci-fi for most people to swallow." She wondered when Gia would get to the part where those long fingers touched her face. She was prepped and ready to file away that particular sensory memory for frequent replays. She might not be the dating type, but she wasn't dead—despite the corpse comment.

"Well, I'm sure there are medical reasons. But it *is* kind

of a scary thought, having little duplicates of yourself running around," Gia said, almost apologetically. She inclined her head. "Please excuse my ignorance if that's a misconception. I don't know much about cloning."

"Don't worry. There's no doubt Hollywood and the special interest groups who oppose us have put skewed impressions out there. It'll be hard for the stodgy science community to overcome."

Gia made a rumble of agreement deep in her throat. "Take your glasses off for me, Emie."

Anything else? she wanted to ask. Her cheeks heated. Jesus. She didn't usually have such wanton thoughts in the midst of a normal conversation. Or—let's face it—ever. Then again, she'd never had a conversation with Gia Mendez before.

Emie watched, mesmerized, as Gia picked up a large, fluffy makeup brush and dipped it into one of the containers. Poofs of face powder launched into the air around the brush, tiny particles dancing in the light. Gia paused, raising perfectly peaked eyebrows, reminding Emie of the request.

Request?

Glasses.

Oh, yeah.

"I'm sorry," she murmured. She removed her frames and folded them in her lap, then closed her eyes while Gia tickled her face with the brush. The sweet fragrance of the mineral powder reminded her fondly of playing dress-up as a child, back when she still hoped—and cared—that she'd grow up beautiful. Before she realized brains were the most beautiful part of a woman anyway. She wanted to smile, but didn't, fearing she'd get that crap in her teeth.

When Gia finished, Emie put her glasses back on and waved her hands to fend off the cloud that still hung in the air. "I just hope the audience is open-minded and not hostile with me. With a topic like this, believe me, it can happen."

Gia stilled. "I…uh, yeah."

A thick pause ensued, prompting a seedling of discomfort to sprout in Emie's middle. Okay, was she missing something here?

"Well, you'll knock 'em dead, I'm sure."

Stop reading into everything, Em. "I hope you're right."

Gia made careful work of capping the mineral powder container and lining up the compacts before looking back at her. "Can I ask you something?"

"Sure."

"Do you ever…watch *The Barry Stillman Show*?"

"Oh, you would ask me that." Emie twisted her mouth to the side apologetically. "I'm ashamed to say that I've never seen it. My work keeps me so busy, I just don't have much time for television."

Gia pressed her full lips into a thin line and nodded.

"Why?" Emie asked.

"I'm…no reason. Just wondering."

It sure sounded like there was a reason behind the "no reason," but Emie didn't want to push. Maybe Gia was just having a bad day. A fight with her undoubtedly fantastic girlfriend at the breakfast table, perhaps. An ugly pang struck Emie at the thought, and her gaze fell to Gia's hands. No rings of any kind. No ring marks. She sighed with relief. As if it mattered. Not all lesbian couples wore rings anyway. And, oh yeah, she wasn't looking! *Get a life, Em.*

"I must say, I'm impressed, though," she told Gia, crossing one leg over the other, bouncing her foot to expel excess nervous energy. "I didn't know any of the talk shows still dealt with legitimate topics these days."

Gia didn't comment, so Emie went on. "If it's not people beating each other up or fake transvestites in love triangles, it never seems to make it to daytime TV. At least, that comprised the sum total of my misconceptions until I was asked on the show." Emie glanced at her reflection, which jolted her back to the matter at hand. She pressed her fingers to her cheeks and pulled down slightly. "Aren't you going to do something with my face? The head camerawoman said I looked like a corpse."

Gia moved in between her and the mirror and spread her legs until she'd lowered herself to Emie's eye level. Emie folded her hands in her lap as her heart thunk-thunked in her chest at the proximity. Wasn't breathing supposed to be automatic? She vaguely recalled that from her high school science classes.

Gia reached for her face slowly. Long, warm fingers danced along her cheekbones, her temples, then she smoothed the pad of her thumb over Emie's chin. "No, Dr. Jaramillo, you don't look like a corpse. Anything but." Her voice was an unexpected gentle caress. "You look beautiful just as you are."

Emie's heart triple-timed. "Well…thank you. And generally, I wouldn't care, but—"

"Just…remember that." Gia touched the end of her nose, the gesture infinitely intimate. "Okay?"

Emie frowned, confused by Gia's words and way too irritatingly spellbound by her touch. "I—sure. But I don't get it. Does that mean you aren't going to make up my face?"

The look Gia gave her seemed almost apologetic. "I'm not going to make up your face. But it's okay. You're a natural beauty. You don't need war paint."

"Tell that to the camera operators." So much for her moment of vanity. Disappointment drizzled over Emie before she shrugged it off and decided Gia was trying to tactfully tell her it wouldn't make much difference. Splashing color on her features would have probably just drawn attention to their plainness. Like a corpse *in* the coffin.

Eh, well, it didn't matter, and she wasn't going to pout about it. This was, after all, how she looked on a normal basis. At least Gia had touched her. Emie inhaled the heady mingled scents of makeup and heated feminine skin, and decided a change of subject was in order.

"How long have you done this kind of work?" Was that relief she saw on the other woman's beautiful face? Why?

"Three long years I've worked on this show." Gia leaned against the counter again, hands spread wide and braced on the edge, and crossed one foot over the other.

"You make it sound like a jail sentence."

Gia tilted her head to the side in a gesture of indifference. "It pays the bills, but my first love…" Doubt crossed her impeccable features. "You want to hear all this?"

"Of course I do, or I wouldn't have asked," Emie assured her. "Your first love?"

"Is painting," Gia finished.

Emie watched in wonder as the smile lit up Gia's face. Her gaze grew distant, dreamy. She hadn't thought Gia could get much more attractive. Boy, had she underestimated the woman. "With war paint?" she teased, glancing back at the mirror.

Gia chuckled. "No, not face painting. Oil painting. Art."

"An artist. Hmm. I'm not surprised." Gia had the hands of an artist, hands that made Emie wish she were a fresh, new canvas ripe for Gia's attention. She could almost feel the brush strokes…

She swallowed. "It's wonderful, Gia. What do you paint?"

"Later." Emie watched a muscle tick in Gia's jaw for several quick moments as her dark eyes grew more serious. With a staccato glance at the door and back, Gia squatted before her and sandwiched one of Emie's icy hands between her own warm ones. "Emie, listen to me. About the show—"

Before Gia could finish, the harried producer knocked sharply, then opened the door a crack and poked her head in. Tendrils had sprung free of her lopsided French twist into which she'd stuck two pencils and apparently forgotten them. "Dr. Jaramillo, time to go on."

Gia stood and moved away, sticking her hands into her back pockets. Regret socked Emie in the stomach, and she pinned Gia with her gaze. What had she been about to say? Absurd as it was,

Emie didn't want to leave this room, this woman. Gia was so comfortable to talk to, and so easy on the eyes. Women like Gia didn't usually orbit Emie's sun. "I—"

"Now, Dr. Jaramillo. Please," the producer urged.

"Go on, Emie," Gia told her, treating her to another devastating wink.

"What were you going to tell me?"

"It's not important. Just, break a leg," she said, her voice husky. "That means good luck." She flashed a thumbs up. "I'll see you again in a few minutes."

Emie peered at Gia curiously as she got out of the chair and smoothed the front of her suit. *A few minutes?* Hope spiked inside her. "You will?"

"I mean...I'll watch you on the monitors."

"Oh." Long awkward pause. "Well. Thank you." She fluffed her own hair with trembling fingers and stuffed back a wave of disappointment. What had she expected? A pledge of undying love? That wasn't even in her life plan, so why now?

With one last smile for Gia and a deep breath for courage, Emie turned and trailed the producer from the room.

❖

"Damnit!" Gia exclaimed as soon as the slim, soft-spoken professor was out of the makeup studio. She slumped into the chair and held her forehead in her hands as guilt assailed her gut. When the door squeaked open, she looked up to find the stage manager, Arlon, peering in at her.

Arlon raised a brow. "What's up?"

"That poor woman has no idea what she's in for," Gia muttered. "This is going to be a nightmare. She honestly thinks she's going to talk about human cloning."

"Ah, you soft touch." Arlon snorted, leaning against the doorjamb with his clipboard cradled in his beefy arms. The remote radio headset nestled on his bald head looked like it had grown there, it was so much a part of the man. "Anyone who agrees to come onto *The Barry Stillman Show* deserves what she gets. You'd have to live in a cave to think this show bore any resemblance to legitimacy."

"She's never *seen* it, Arlon. She's never even heard the buzz." Gia lunged to her feet and stalked across the small room. She punched the Stop button on the iPod dock, then braced her palms against the wall and hung her head. Emie Jaramillo had infiltrated her domain all of what—ten minutes? And already Mary J.'s "Sweet Thing" reminded her of Emie. Gia could still smell her lavender scent in the air.

God, she felt like a heel.

That sweet, intelligent woman with the heart-shaped face and trusting eyes didn't deserve this ambush. Gia had expected a renowned young scientist to be arrogant and aloof. Haughty, at the very least. Instead, Emie had turned out to be one of the most down-to-earth, reachable women she'd met in a long time. From her inquisitive brown eyes hidden behind those endearing spectacles to her joking manner and wide smile, Emie was nothing if not genuine.

"Sure, she's seen it." Arlon's skeptical voice cut into Gia's thoughts. "Everyone's seen *The Barry Stillman Show*."

"Not everyone spends their days propped in front of the boob tube, Arlon. She's a scientist. She has a life. An all-consuming career."

He whistled low. "She's got you all worked up, Mendez. Must've been some looker. No, wait"—Arlon turned his attention to the clipboard he held—"she couldn't be a looker if she's on *this* particular episode. My mistake."

"She looked great. Gorgeous," Gia snapped, whirling toward her colleague. With effort, she stopped, and ran her palms down her face, willing herself to relax. "I'm sorry. I don't mean to take it out on you."

"It's all good." Arlon pushed off the doorjamb and moved closer. "What's really up?"

Gia blew out a breath. "Doesn't it ever get to you, Arlon? Lying to these people just to get them on the show?"

He considered the question, then shrugged. "It's just a job, G. Television. Mindless entertainment—emphasis on the mindless part. Besides, you were just the makeup artist in the whole thing. She can't blame you."

"But she will, that's the thing. She'll think we all lied to her, and we *did*. To her"—Gia pointed in the general direction of the stage—"this will be a public shaming." She clenched her jaw, fighting back those familiar regret-laden feelings from her past. If anyone in this world did not deserve to be bullied, it was Dr. Emie Jaramillo. "We're sending an innocent lamb to the slaughter. How can we live with ourselves?"

"I get your point, Gia, but seriously, lay off the melodrama. So the lady gets embarrassed on television. Big deal. She'll get over it."

Gia burned him a glare. So jaded. So cavalier.

"Besides, there's nothing we can do about it now," Arlon added, pressing the earphone tighter to his ear. "Looks like the good professor just went on."

The whoops and hollers from the audience surprised Emie as she walked onstage and took a seat in one of the two chairs centered on the carpeted platform. She'd expected a more demure group for a show about the scientific and medical aspects of cloning, but at least they seemed welcoming. Behind her, an elaborate set gave the appearance of a comfortable living room. Lights mounted on scaffolding glared in her eyes, but she could vaguely make out the faces in the tiered crowd seated in a semicircle before her.

After settling into her chair, she gazed around the audience searching for her family and friends. There they were, front and center. Mama, Papa, Iris, and Paloma, all in a row.

She smiled at them, but they looked odd.

Paloma's hands were clasped at her ample bosom, her eyes wide and serious. And Iris? Emie could swear she looked flaming mad. Come to think of it, her father looked a little angry himself. Was Mama crying?

Perplexed, Emie squinted out at them. Yes, Mama was definitely crying. Had something bad happened since the last time she spoke to them? She fought the urge to traverse the stage and find out for herself. Her adrenaline level kicked up a notch. Before she could worry further, the raucous cheering died down, and Barry Stillman smiled at her from the aisle where he stood.

"Dr. Jaramillo, welcome to the show."

"Thank you," she murmured, pushing up her glasses with her knuckle. Laughter rippled through the audience, which confused her.

"Tell us a little about your research, Doctor."

She crossed one leg over the other and leaned forward. Her confidence always jumped when she could discuss her studies. She favored her host with an enthusiastic smile. "Well, I'm a professor of genetics engineering at a private college in Colorado. We're leading the country's research into cloning. Particularly human cloning, though the procedure is still quite controversial in the United States."

"Sounds like a job that could keep a woman pretty busy."

Apprehension began to claw its way up her spine. She glanced at the empty chair next to her and wondered who should be sitting there. They hadn't told her she would be part of a panel. And what was with Barry's inane questions? She licked her dry lips, wishing for water. "Yes, it's exhausting work."

"Probably doesn't leave you too much time for pampering, Dr. Jaramillo, does it?" More laughter spattered through the crowd.

Suddenly defensive, Emie sat back in her chair and crossed her arms to match her entwined legs. Her skin flamed, and a rivulet of perspiration rolled down her stiff spine. "Forgive my confusion. I thought we were going to discuss human cloning." This time, the audience remained silent, but the pause seemed packed with gunpowder and about to explode.

"Well, Dr. Jaramillo, we aren't going to discuss human cloning. We actually have a surprise for you."

Emie blinked several times, trying to grasp what was happening to her. She glanced off into the wings and saw Gia standing there, her dark eyes urgent and pained. Their gazes met momentarily before Gia hung her head and turned away.

What in the hell was going on?

"Surprise?" Emie finally croaked out. "I don't understand."

"Maybe we can help you understand. Listen to this audio tape, Doctor, for a clue about who brought you on today's show."

Everyone fell silent, and soon a deep, accented, patronizing voice boomed through the studio. "Emie, I know you want me. But I'm here to tell you, before we have a chance, your bookworm looks have *got* to go. I'm doing this for your own good."

Realization filtered through Emie's disbelief like acid burning through her flesh. The phone sex voice belonged to none other than Vitoria Elizalde, her barracuda Brazilian coworker who refused to take no for an answer. Emie covered her mouth with her hand as the words slithered through her brain. *I've been duped!*

Emie had gone for coffee with Vitoria twice in the past month, purely as a gesture of professional respect. Vitoria was a visiting researcher from a different country, and though Emie found her insufferably arrogant and conceited, even predatory, she'd tried her damnedest to make Vitoria feel welcome on the team. Of course a cretin like Vitoria would assume a few goddamn cups of coffee meant Emie wanted more. Typical. This was exactly why Emie had chosen not to date. Ever.

As the audience roared their approval, the host asked her, "Recognize that voice, Doctor?"

She couldn't even nod, let alone speak. First comparing

her to a corpse, and now bookworm looks? Mortification spiked Emie to her seat as her heart sank. Hot tears stung her eyes, and as her chin started to quiver, the audience burst into applause, chanting, "Bar-ry! Bar-ry! Bar-ry! Bar-ry!"

She glanced out at her supporters, who looked as horrified as she felt. Iris mouthed the words, "I'm so sorry."

Stillman's obnoxious voice cut in with, "Audience, what's your vote?" after which a hundred or more black placards were thrust into the air. SHE'S A BOOKWORM, most of them read, in neon yellow lettering. Belatedly, Papa lifted his sign to its neon yellow flipside with shaky, liver-spotted hands. SHE'S A BEAUTY, spelled the stark black lettering. Emie was so ashamed for putting her parents into this humiliating position. If only she'd known it was all a trick—

"Audience? What do you have to say to Dr. Jaramillo?"

A hundred collective voices yelled at her, "Don't worry, Bookworm. We're going to make you over!"

Emie saw stars, and gripped the chair arms so she wouldn't faint. What a nightmare. No wonder Gia didn't make up her face. She wasn't beautiful, like Gia had claimed. Rather, all of them—Gia included—wanted her to look her very worst when she walked onto this stage. Emie choked back a sob. For some reason, Gia's deception cut to her core. The beautiful makeup artist had seemed so sincere. It had felt as if they'd made a connection. *Fooled you, Emie.*

"Welcome Professor Vitoria Elizalde to the show!" Barry hollered. From out of the wings opposite where she'd seen Gia sauntered smug, pantherlike Vitoria, her black hair perfectly coiffed. She raised her arms to the audience like a reigning queen as they clapped and cheered for her. She even took a bow.

How could she do this?

How could she bring Emie on national television, in front of God and her parents, friends? Everyone. Her staff, their colleagues. What the hell was wrong with this psycho bitch?

Before Emie could stop them, hot tears burst forth behind

her glasses and blurred her vision. As Vitoria took the empty chair next to her, Emie lunged unsteadily to her feet and backed away, smearing at the tears rolling down her makeup-free face. She tore the lavalier microphone from her lapel and tossed it aside, then laid her palms on her flat, trembling abdomen.

"How could you, Vitoria? You stupid, arrogant bitch," she rasped, before wheeling on her comfortable, sensible heels and running from the stage trailed by the audience's loud booing.

Offstage, the producer with pencils in her hair caught Emie by her upper arms and held her back. "Come now, Emie. They're going to give you a makeover. It won't be so bad."

Her tears had escalated to sobs, which had prompted hiccups. Were these people for real? "Leave me—" *hiccup* "—alone. I'm not going back out—" *hiccup* "—there. Now or ever."

She tried to push past the woman when another man arrived to assist. The producer glanced at the man for help. "Arlon?"

"Don't, uh, cry now, miss," the man said, his stilted words proving him ill at ease with the role of comforter. He patted her upper arm and cleared his throat. "It's not so bad. We'll just get you some ice for your puffy eyes and—"

"Let. Her. Go," Gia's dead serious voice said from behind Emie. "Now."

Both the producer and the man called Arlon diverted their attention to Gia, and Emie took advantage of the moment to push between them and run through the cables and scaffolding to the hallway that would lead her out. Behind her, she heard the producer say, "Stay out of this, Mendez."

Emie wept freely, never so embarrassed in all her life.

She'd worked so hard to make her parents proud. They'd brought her to the U.S. from Mexico when she was a toddler, hoping to provide her with better opportunities. They'd given up everything familiar—their family, friends, the language they both spoke so eloquently, the country they loved—for her. Her entire life was geared to show them her gratitude, to show them she'd made the most of their sacrifices to become a success, a daughter of whom they could be truly proud. Now this.

Sure, she was a well-educated woman, a leader in her field, but she couldn't help thinking Mama and Papa had seen her in another light today. As a homely thirty-year-old woman who didn't even merit a date with an overblown, cocksure player in whom she'd never be the least bit interested. She'd never focused on appearance, but this idiotic show had thrown her supposed shortcomings into sharp relief.

She shoved against the bar spanning the metal door and pushed her way into the exit hallway and wondered how she'd ever live this down, how she'd ever make it up to the parents who valued their dignity so.

"Emie! Wait!"

Gia. Emie tried to keep running, to get away before she ever had to see the woman's lying face again, but Gia caught her and snaked a hand around her forearm.

"Let me go," she said, staring at the ground as she tried to wrench free. Part of her wished Gia would just hold her and tell her everything would be okay. *The stupid part of me that didn't even exist before today, before that damned makeup room.*

"Emie, please. I'm so sorry. Listen, let me ex—"

"Sorry?" Fury mixed with her humiliation as she hiccupped again. Gia had pretended to be nice to her, when all the while she'd been part of the lie. "You think that weightless word makes it all better? Leave me alone, Gia, okay?"

Emie lifted her chin, pushed up her glasses, and glared, trying her best to mask the hurt with a look of indignance. She yanked her arm from Gia's grasp and rubbed the spot she'd held with her other hand. Her chest heaved as she stared up at the woman she'd trusted, the woman she'd lusted after, if only for a short time. The woman who'd played a major part in the biggest humiliation of her life.

"I want to explain."

"Yeah? And I don't want to hear it. I want you to back the hell off. After all this, can't you—" *hiccup* "—at least do that?" She turned and stumbled slowly down the long, stark corridor. Her limbs felt leaden, like all the energy had been leached out of her. She just wanted to go home and put sweats on and curl up with a glass of—

"I meant what I said, Emie," Gia called after her. "You are amazingly beautiful."

Her heart clenched. *Another lie.*

Emie never even turned back.

CHAPTER TWO

Telling the Barry Stillman people to take their job and shove it hadn't been difficult for Gia. But packing up her worldly goods and driving across the country in search of a woman she'd met but once, a woman who haunted her dreams— and probably hated her guts—was the biggest risk she'd ever taken.

No matter. It felt good. She'd been on the road for at least twelve hours, and as the evening skyline of Denver loomed into sight, Gia glanced down at the directions she hoped would lead her to Emie. The doctor deserved an apology, and for maybe the first time in her life, Gia would do everything she could to make things right with a person she'd hurt who hadn't deserved it. She steered her black pickup onto Speer Blvd. South and moved to the center lane. Rolling down her window, she breathed in the cool, dry summertime air that was so different from the stifling humidity in Chicago where she'd grown up. Then again, everything about growing up had been stifling for her.

It was almost as hard for Gia to remember herself as an angry young bully as it was to remind herself she wasn't one anymore. She'd transformed, and she had her high school art teacher, Mr. Fuentes, to thank for her changed demeanor. Though rail thin and openly, proudly effeminate, Fuentes wouldn't be bullied. He'd never once flinched when he faced the angry young Gia toe-to-toe, and yet he never made her feel worthless, either. On the contrary, Fuentes made Gia believe in her painting, in her talent. He'd shown her how to channel all that pent-up rage into art and made her understand that true happiness came from inside a person, not outside. Even though Gia hadn't gotten to the point where she could fully support herself with her painting, she'd had a couple of shows, made a few sales, and, at age thirty-four, she still believed in herself.

Fuentes had won Gia's respect, later her admiration. She'd thanked the man on more than one occasion over the years, but she'd never gone back and outright apologized to any of the people she'd bullied and hurt. Perhaps a turned-around life was penance enough, but the open-ended guilt of her youth hung around her heart like an anchor. She might not be able to assuage it with one apology, but it was a step in the right direction. And any steps that carried her closer to Dr. Emie Jaramillo were ones she definitely wanted to take.

If she was honest with herself, it wasn't just the chance to set things right that led her to the slight professor with the short, silky hair that just begged a woman to run her fingers through it. Something far more instinctual pulled her as well. It had taken one fitful night of remembering Emie's gentle lavender scent, seeing images of her bright, dark eyes behind those glasses, hearing her wind-chime laughter, before Gia knew she had to see Emie again. If she didn't, Emie's memory would be with her forever, like a war wound. Reminding her now and then, with a stab of pain, what could possibly have been.

She glanced back down at the crinkled map in the passenger seat, brushing aside the wadded Snickers wrappers covering it. If her navigation was correct, she should be knocking on Emie's door in no time. And, if fate was on her side, the doc would be willing to hear her out.

❖

Three hellish days had passed since the ill-fated appearance on *The Barry Stillman Show*. Emie—bundled in voluminous sweatpants and feeling like lukewarm death—slumped cross-legged on the floor of her living room across from her best buddies, Iris Lujan and Paloma Vargas. Between them, on the dark brown patterned area rug, sat serving dishes filled with various comfort foods: enchilada casserole, mashed potatoes, chicken mole, and a half-frozen Sara Lee cheesecake. Not to mention the pitcher of margaritas. Their forks hung limply from their hands as they took a collective break from gastronomically comforting themselves.

Emie leaned back against her slip-covered sofa and laid her hands on her distended abdomen with a groan. If only Gia Mendez could see her at this moment, she thought acidly. How beautiful would the makeup artist claim she was now?

Emie's eyes were still tear-swollen, and she'd broken out in a rash on her neck from the stress. Her hair was smashed on one side, spiked out on the other, since she'd spent most of the last two days lying listlessly on the couch channel-surfing through shows she didn't know a thing about (ah, the irony) to kill time between her crying jags. Now she was bloated, and she simply didn't care. The entire TV-watching universe was already focused on her appearance rather than her groundbreaking scientific work. No sense trying to "pretty up."

Oddly enough, a memory far removed from her being humiliated on television kept popping into her mind, squeezing her heart. She'd been just a little girl, one who loved playing dress-up and watching Miss Universe on TV. She would close her eyes during commercials and picture herself accepting the crown for the USA in English, then thanking her parents in Spanish. At that point, she still believed it could happen. At that point, she still *wanted* it to happen.

But one summer afternoon, her aunt Luz and her mother were sharing iced tea on the front porch while Emie played with dolls in her room. Her window was open, inviting a breeze that carried the voices of Mama and Tía Luz.

"Look, Luz. Photographs of the children from the church picnic last week."

The sounds of Tía Luz thumbing through the prints came next, and Emie's ears perked when she heard, "Ah, there's little Emie." A pause. "Such a smart girl."

"*Gracias,*" murmured her mother, and Emie could hear the smile on Mama's face.

"Thank God for her brains. She certainly didn't get the looks. With those skinny chicken knees and thick glasses, she may never find a husband, but she'll always find a good job."

Emie froze, a crampy feeling in her stomach like when she'd eaten too much raw cookie dough the week before. She set down her dolls and curled up on her side on the floor, hoping her tummy would stop hurting. It made her want to cry. She tried to stop listening, but she couldn't help herself.

Her mama tsk-tsked. "Don't be cruel, Luz. Not everyone can be beautiful, nor does everyone need a husband. She'll grow into her looks."

"We can only hope she's a late bloomer," Tía Luz added.

But she hadn't bloomed at all, no matter what Gia had claimed about her looks. If she had, she wouldn't have ended up as a guest on Barry Stillman's horrific bookworm makeover show. And after that day, hearing Tía Luz's unintentionally cruel comments, she'd stopped caring about society's notion of beauty, stopped watching Miss Universe. She focused instead on academics and eschewed the notion of ever finding someone to love. This wasn't the damned Ark; people didn't have to live in pairs. And she'd been happy. Perfectly satisfied with the life she'd built…until that asshole Barry Stillman came into her life. Still, the memory of that long-ago day hurt as if fresh. She pushed it from her mind, scratched at the red bumps below her ear, and hiccuped.

"You still have those?" Paloma asked.

"I get them when I'm under—"*hiccup*"—stress." She nudged up her glasses, then took to scratching the other side of her neck. "They've come and gone since the—" *hiccup* "—fiasco. I'm probably just gulping—" *hiccup* "—down my food too fast."

Paloma got up, stepped over the smorgasbord, then plopped herself onto the couch behind Emie. "I'm gonna plug your ears, and you drink your margarita. It may not get rid of 'em, but after all that tequila, you won't care."

Emie let out a mirthless chuckle, then did as she was told. It worked. She smiled up at Paloma, who'd begun playing with Emie's unruly hair, and absentmindedly brought her fingernails to her neck again.

"Honey, don't scratch your rash. You'll make it worse," Iris told her softly. "Did you use that cream I gave you?"

Emie nodded and rested her hands in her lap. If anyone knew what being judged for one's looks felt like, it was Iris. She and Emie understood the concept from different perspectives, though. Iris, a natural beauty with wavy, waist-length black hair and huge green eyes, had gone on to a great modeling career after being named Prettiest Girl in high school. At thirty, she was one of America's most recognizable Chicanas, having graced the pages of *Cosmo*, *Vanity Fair*, *Latina*, *Vanidades*, and *Vogue*, to name a few. In looks, she and Emie were polar opposites, always had been. But in their hearts, along with Paloma, they were soul triplets.

If only I'd looked like Iris onstage. Maybe then Gia would have felt something for her other than pity. Iris never lacked in attention from gorgeous women.

No.

No.

That's not who Emie was, nor who she wanted to be. And *The Barry Stillman Show* damn well wasn't going to shake the core of her self-esteem.

Emie closed her eyes against a fresh wave of embarrassment

as she relived, yet again, the now infamous filming fiasco in Chicago. On the airplane home, she'd felt as if everyone was staring at her. *Look! There's the bookworm professor!*

The mere thought that she'd been internalizing such superficial crap demoralized her. She'd self-medicated with several tiny bottles of cheap screw-cap wine during the flight, and had finally convinced herself that not only was she being overly paranoid, but she didn't care. Still, it had taken every ounce of her courage to walk through Denver International Airport with her head held up, even with Iris and Paloma flanking her for much-needed moral support. Of course people had seen her. *The Barry Stillman Show* had 30 million viewers, she'd since learned via a Google search. She just wasn't sure *who* had seen her, and that's what scared her most.

It had felt so good to finally walk into her comfortable home in Washington Park and deadbolt the door behind her. And after a half hour of quiet, she'd started to feel better, thinking maybe no one *had* seen the show. Then her phone had begun to ring. It seemed everyone she'd ever met in her life had seen the goddamn show. Her voicemail had been clogged for two days with uncomfortable messages of sympathy and pity—just what she needed. A local full-service beauty salon had even sent a courier bearing a gift certificate, much to her utter dismay.

The phone rang again, and Emie glared at it. "I swear, I could kill that thing," she whispered to her friends, chugging down another healthy dose of margarita. She wiped salt from her lips and added, "Who could that be now? The president? I think he's the only one who hasn't sent condolences for the untimely death of my dignity."

Iris clicked her tongue and cast a beseeching look at Emie while Paloma reached over and switched off the ringer. "When we realized what they were doing, we tried our hardest to get backstage to warn you, Emie, I swear," Iris told her, for the millionth time.

"They wouldn't let us," Paloma added, digging her fork into

the cheesecake. "Rat bastards. Your mama laid into them with a barrage of Spanish cuss words unlike anything I've ever heard before. Made my hair stand on end. I think they didn't know quite what to do with her." She popped the bite into her mouth and chewed, her eyes fixed apologetically on Emie's face.

"I don't blame you guys. I just wish someone in my circle of friends watched that ridiculous show so I could've had some warning. It was my fault for walking into their trap." She furrowed her fingers into her hair and laid her head back against the couch. And what a trap they'd set, with a juicy enticer like Gia Mendez to lure women in. Or men, for that matter. She couldn't imagine a soul on earth who wouldn't find Gia Mendez sexy. *God, I'm so stupid.*

"It's unconscionable what they do to people, Emie. You should complain," Iris said, dishing up another serving of enchiladas.

She shook thoughts of Gia from her mind and graced her friend with a wan smile. "Eh, it wouldn't do any good. Besides, I just want to forget it ever happened." *To forget that I entertained even one thought that a sex goddess like Gia Mendez would look twice at a lab rat like me.*

"How much time off do you have before the new semester starts?" Paloma asked.

"A little over a month." A little over four weeks until she had to face Vile Vitoria again. The thought of Elizalde made her want to fistfight. "God, that arrogant whore," she said. "Who does she think she is, anyway?"

"That's right," Paloma said, wrapping her arms around Emie's shoulders from behind for a hug. "As if you'd ever give her the time of day."

Emie didn't think she'd go that far, but she only said, "I've got to think of some way to get back at her."

"Oh, revenge." Iris nodded. "That's always a good, healthy way to recover from trauma."

Recognizing the sarcasm, Emie rolled her eyes. "In any case,

I'm hoping by the time I go back it will be old news to everyone and my own embarrassment will have waned. I want absolutely no reminders of that debacle." *Especially none of a brown-eyed artist with fingers that could make a woman scream for edible body paints.*

The doorbell chimed. Twice.

Emie looked from Iris to Paloma and frowned. "Who could that be? *TMZ?*"

"Very funny. It's probably your mama," Iris said, standing. "I'll get it."

"No, wait." Emie groaned to her feet. "Let me. It'll probably be the only exercise I get all week." Padding across the room in a tequila-induced zigzag, Emie made her way to the dark front hall leading to the door. Lord knew, she needed some fresh air.

July in Colorado heated right up, but the temperature dropped with the sun, bringing cool breezes in with the moon. Maybe she'd sit with Mama on the porch instead of bringing her inside. The darkness would hide some of the puffiness around her eyes, and staying outside would prevent Mama from witnessing their little pity party on the living room carpet. Mama would be aghast that they were eating so much food from dishes set right on the floor. She was nothing if not proper.

Emie stopped in the dark hallway, leaned against the wall, and pulled in a long, deep breath. Just the thought of seeing her mother brought on renewed feelings of shame. Oh, her parents had handled everything much better than she had. It didn't matter—she still felt guilty. She knew, deep down, they had to be embarrassed that their daughter wound up in such a shameful public position. No matter how long it took, she was going to put the incident to rest for all of them, just as soon as her anger at Vitoria Elizalde dissipated.

Emie flipped on the porch light before she threw the deadbolt back and pulled on the heavy, carved wooden door. She started speaking as the hinges squeaked.

"It's late, Mama, you shouldn't be ou—" Her words cut

off as her mind grasped the realization that the lean, muscular woman looming larger than life on her porch bore no resemblance whatsoever to her mother.

Emie wasn't sure if her heart had stopped or was beating so fast she couldn't feel it. Either way, she looked like hell and had a guacamole smear on her sweatshirt, and here she stood face-to-face with— "Gia—" *hiccup* "—w-what are you doing here?" Amazingly calm question considering her life had just passed before her eyes. Emie hoped she wouldn't fall down, because she could no longer feel her feet. And, physiological impossibility aside, she'd just proven that a person could exist without a heartbeat or the ability to draw air into the lungs.

Gia Mendez? HERE?

"Emie. Forgive me for…just showing up." She spread her arms wide and let them drop to her sides, as if searching for what to say next. Her long, silky hair hung free of the ponytail Emie remembered, and the yellow glow of the porch light made it shine like a sheet of black gold. Gia looked just as good in dark jeans and a well-worn University of Chicago sweatshirt as she had the day Emie'd met her in her Stillman work attire.

Looking at her, Emie fought the ridiculous urge to sit on the floor. Instead, she stood stock still and bunched the avocado-stained front of her sweatshirt into her fist. With her other hand, she poked her glasses up on her nose. "I…I thought I made it clear you should—" *hiccup* "—leave me alone."

To her dismay, Gia flashed a devastating, sweet smile that pulled a dimple into her left cheek. Emie hadn't noticed that the other day. "Don't tell me you've had those hiccups since you left Chicago."

She shook her head and hiccuped again.

"Emie, we need to talk." Gia took a step forward, and Emie eased the door partway closed, hiding half of her body behind it. Gia stopped, stared at her. Her gaze dropped to Emie's neck as she swallowed.

"No," Emie said. "We don't need to talk. I want to"—she

held her breath for a moment and staved off a hiccup—"forget everything about that day." God, she wanted to be angry at Gia Mendez. She didn't want to feel her heart beating in anticipation at the mere sight of her, or worry that Gia had noticed her disheveled hair. She didn't want to smell the woman's pheromones on the night air or yearn to feel Gia's strong arms around her for comfort. "Denial is my drug of choice. I'm going to pretend it never happened."

"It shouldn't have happened, Emie." Gia laid her palm high up on the door frame, leaning toward her. "I feel just—"

"Don't." Emie held out her hand. Attraction or not, Gia had been a part of the ruse; Emie couldn't forget that. "Don't apologize now, after the fact, because I really, really thought you were a nice woman, Gia Mendez. An apology will only make me want to slug you, and I've had too much trauma and too much—" *hiccup* "—tequila to resist the urge."

Gia paused to chew on her full, sexy lip. "It's a risk I'm willing to take."

Her pointed gaze, filled with inexplicable affection, flamed Emie's cheeks. She expelled a sigh and hung her head. How much could one woman take? It had been a long time since her Tía Luz had pointed out her flaws, and though her glasses weren't as thick these days, her knees were just as knobby. She couldn't let a woman like Gia, a woman solidly out of her league, affect the way she looked at herself or led her life. It would only bring her more pain. After a moment, she raised her gaze. "Look. You were only doing your job, okay? I understand."

Gia opened her mouth to speak, but Emie waved her words away, reminding herself to be angry. Gia had tricked her. She'd shamed her. She'd left her face corpse-bare, even knowing what kind of trap Emie was walking into. "It's fine, Gia, please. Just… leave me to my life and go back to yours. There are a lot of other *Stillman Show* guests to dupe, I'm sure."

"Emie?" called Iris from the front room. "You okay?"

"Fine," she yelled back, a little too sharply, her eyes never leaving Gia's face.

"Slug me if you want, but I *am* sorry. More than you'll ever know. You probably don't believe that."

"Did you come here to convince me or yourself? Because you've already told me one lie. You'll have a tough job on your hands if you're working on me."

"Emie," Gia breathed her name, a pained gaze imploring.

Gia didn't try to touch her. Emie didn't try to move away. Time stilled between them as they stared at one another. Gia dipped her chin, Emie raised hers. Crickets chirped from the darkness beyond the porch. A gust of wind rustled the leaves on her old grand oak tree and lifted a lock of Gia's long hair across her face.

"Why are you here?" Emie whispered. "You live in Chicago."

"Used to live in Chicago." Gia tucked her hair behind one ear. "I don't work for *The Stillman Show* anymore."

"You don't?"

"You *are* an attractive woman, Emie." The words came out husky. "A beautiful woman. I mean it."

Emie ignored that. If *that's* what Gia thought she'd been worrying about, she was greatly mistaken. Plus, Emie had more pressing questions. "Did you get fired?"

"Quit."

Surprise fluttered through her and she let go of the door. "Why?" she asked, moving closer to lean against the jamb.

"Because I never again wanted to see hurt on a person's face like I saw on yours as you left the studio. I can't stop the show from bringing people on under false pretenses, but I can sure as hell remove myself from the situation."

Emie sighed and broke eye contact, focusing instead on Gia's low-heeled black boots. Why did she have to be so freaking nice? So sincere? Why couldn't she leave Emie to her sulking instead of invading her doorstep with her stature and warmth, filling Emie's nostrils with the feminine scent of her skin and her ears with that silky-husky voice? "I can't feel responsible for you losing your job, Gia."

"I'm not blaming you."

She raised her gaze back to Gia's. "What will you do?"

Gia shrugged. "I'll get by. It's time to give my painting a chance, and…who knows?"

Emie shook her head slowly and reached up to scratch her neck. Gia had quit her job. She'd quit her job and packed up her life, and now she was standing on Emie's doorstep hundreds of miles away trying to convince her she wasn't unattractive.

Why?

Feeling another bout of hiccups coming on, Emie whispered, "I have to go."

"Can I come in?"

"No." She started to shut the door.

Gia held it open. "Emie, wait. I want to see you again."

"To assuage your own guilt? I don't think so."

"That's not why."

So she said. But, really, how would Emie ever know?

Gia reached out and ran the backs of those lovely fingers slowly down her cheek. "You have a rash."

"Adds to the whole package, wouldn't you say?"

"Don't, *querida*." Gia's hand slid from Emie's cheek to her shoulder and rested there.

Emie's eyes fluttered shut, and she choked back another wave of tears. This woman could break her heart if she allowed it. "Leave me alone, Gia. Please."

"I can't."

"Emie?" Iris and Paloma peered into the hallway, then looked from their friend to Gia, then eyes widening in surprise. Neither moved.

Emie glanced over her shoulder. "I'll be right there. Ms. Mendez was just leaving."

"No, I wasn't."

"You are now."

"We aren't finished."

"We never even started."

Gia pressed her infinitely kissable lips together and lowered her chin. Her somber gaze melted into Emie's for excruciating seconds before a smile teased that dimple into making an appearance. She winked. "Tomorrow? Can I see you then?"

"No."

"Just coffee. No pressure."

"No."

Gia shifted from boot to boot, then crossed her arms over her chest. "Need I remind you that you said you thought I was a nice woman?"

"I also said I wanted to hit you," she countered, in as haughty a tone as she could muster.

"But you didn't."

Emie faltered and bit her lip, which had started to tremble. "Don't do this to me. Please."

"I'm going to keep trying until you give me a chance."

Shoring up her resolve, Emie wrapped her arms around her stomach and sniffed. "I'm not looking for new friends, and I have no space for a woman in my life. You'll be wasting your time."

Gia brushed Emie's trembling bottom lip with one knuckle, then stepped back. "Ah, but you see, I'd rather waste my time on you than spend it wisely on anyone else." She nodded good night to Iris and Paloma, who still hung behind Emie, then stepped off the porch and disappeared into the night shadows.

The standoff was only temporary; Emie knew that. Though she'd never admit it, she couldn't wait to see what would come next.

CHAPTER THREE

Emie slept fitfully for the next two nights and spent her waking hours answering Iris's and Paloma's never-ending questions about Gia. The whole thing amounted to pure torture. She really didn't want to face the answers. *Who is she? When did you meet? Why is she here? Did she ask you out?* And the Bermuda Triangle of all questions—*How do you feel about her?*

And just how did she feel about Gia? She'd been angry with her and everyone from *The Barry Stillman Show* for a couple days, but she just couldn't drum up that emotion for Gia anymore. She'd apologized, after all, and Emie wasn't a grudge-holding person by nature.

Sure, she was attracted to Gia. Big deal. She was attracted to Jada Pinkett Smith, too, but that didn't mean she'd ever have a chance with the actress or act on that attraction if the world tilted on its axis and such a chance arose. Her feelings about Gia were as jumbled and off balance as her feelings about herself, and it wasn't getting much better.

It didn't help that she hadn't seen hide nor hair of Gia since the night on the porch and couldn't stop wondering if Gia's guilt had dissipated enough for her to just move on. Secretly, the notion disappointed Emie. She didn't want to get her hopes up, didn't want to think about Gia like some obsessive schoolgirl, but she couldn't help it. Gia Mendez had found one of the very few cracks in her shell and invaded her soul. The worst part of that was, Emie wouldn't be with her now even if Gia got down on her knees and begged. She couldn't, not after the Stillman fiasco, knowing she was just a retribution date to Gia and always would be. If they'd met any other way…things might be different.

But they hadn't, and they weren't.

End of story.

Sometime on the second day, Emie had decided hard work was the perfect antidote for what ailed her, and she'd asked Paloma and Iris to help her tackle a project she'd been putting off for far too long: painting her house. Now there they stood, with the morning sun warming their right sides, covering their hair with baseball caps and mixing the paint that Emie hoped would help brighten her house as well as her outlook. And, naturally, they were talking about Gia—the woman who was there even when she *wasn't*, it seemed.

"Of course she's interested in you, Emie, don't be obtuse," said Iris. She held the paint-spraying contraption in her arms like a machine gun, her short but impeccably manicured nails curving around the deadly barrel.

Emie eyed her, wondering if she'd chosen the wrong task for them to undertake. "Your obtuse is my realistic. But no sense quibbling over semantics. Besides, who ever said I wanted a woman in my life at all? Put that paint gun down, you're scaring me." None of them had ever painted a house exterior before, but the old place had been begging for a fresh coat for two summers. If she ever planned on collecting a decent rent for her carriage house apartment, she supposed she'd better pretty up the place.

"Seriously, Em, why else would a woman quit her job, for God's sake, and drive across the country?" Paloma asked.

"Guilt is a powerful motivator," Emie reminded them, flipping her cap around so the bill faced backwards. "It's tough to live with."

"That's a cop-out."

"Well, cop-out or not," Emie said, "she hasn't been back. A woman like Gia Mendez would not base life decisions on a woman like me. And I don't care anyway, so drop it."

Iris, who'd thankfully surrendered her paint weapon, stopped buttoning an oversized Rockies baseball jersey over her shorts and tank top and cast a sardonic glare at Emie. "A woman like you. Hmm. Let's think about that." She propped her fists on her hips and tilted her head to the side in thought. "You're a successful genetics researcher at the ripe young age of thirty, leading the nation's studies into one of the hugest scientific breakthroughs since…since—"

"Turkey basters?" offered Paloma, glancing at her two sons, Pep and Teddy, content to be playing with their prized Matchbox cars on the sidewalk. The boys, like their other mom, were crazy about vehicles and quite knowledgeable about make and model.

"I was going to say Velcro. Or airbrush makeup. But yeah, okay. Since turkey basters." Iris spread her arms and leaned forward, raising her perfectly arched eyebrows at Emie. "You're right, girl. You are a booby prize."

Emie expelled a pointed sigh. "You know what I meant. I'm not saying I'm not successful in my field, nor that I'm not completely content with it. But people are shallow. Given the choice between a lab coat and some sexy"—she spun her hand—"something, which do you think a woman like Gia would choose?"

"You underestimate yourself, Emie, you always have," Paloma said. She gestured down at her very curvy body. "Look at yourself compared to me. You're willowy—"

"Bony."

"And tall—"

"Five-foot-eleven Iris is tall, Paloma. I hate to tell you, but I'm only five-four, and that isn't tall."

"It is when you're four-foot-eleven and chubby."

"You're not chubby, you're voluptuous." Emie sighed and nudged her glasses up. "You two can't possibly understand. Iris, well, you're Iris Lujan. Need I say more? And, Paloma, everyone has loved you since high school. Women *and* men. You're Miss Popularity. I don't remember you ever without a girlfriend."

"Big whoop. I've only had one, and I married her."

"At least you had the choice." Emie clasped her hands together and pleaded with her friends. "No. Forget that. Too 'poor me,' and that's not how I feel. I love my life. Please don't feel like you have to sugarcoat things for me, you two. I'm not saying I begrudge you your beauty, Iris, or your popularity, Paloma. But I need your honesty right now. I'm not denying I'm smart or successful, but—shallow or not—that's not enough salve for the Stillman sting at the moment. You know it's never been that big an issue that I'm not beautiful. Not my focus. We get what we're given and make the best of it. But I was just publicly outed as a hopeless hag on national television." Emie huffed a humorless half-laugh and shook her head. "Forgive me if I wish—just once—that I was at least pretty. Maybe even sexy. Just for a day. Long enough to make Vitoria eat her heart out. Or, I don't know, *die* a painful death."

Iris expelled a little snort.

Paloma just sighed. "You underestimate yourself. I'll say it again. Gia Mendez is hot for you, girl."

A frisson of thrill spiraled through Emie, but she shoved it away. Maybe they wouldn't admit that she wasn't sorely lacking in the prettiness department, but they *had* to admit Gia was out of her league. "Get real. You saw the woman, didn't you?"

"Hell yeah, we saw her," Paloma said. "And if I wasn't married—"

"Or I wasn't in a semi-committed relationship kind of thing," added Iris.

"We'd be fighting your tall, willowy butt for her right here in the yard." Paloma grinned.

Emie smiled back, then bent over to stir the Spring Eggshell all-weather paint, which looked exactly like apple cake batter.

She knew two things for sure. First, everyone, including her two best friends, must think she was either gullible or blind. And second, despite their idle threats, neither Iris nor Paloma would ever go after Gia knowing how she felt about the woman.

Emie stopped stirring and blinked several times.

What was she thinking?

There was that feelings stuff again. She didn't *feel* any way about Gia. She had her pride, for God's sake. She would never accept a pity date, which was precisely all she'd ever get out of Gia Mendez. The woman felt sorry for her. Period. The thought made her cringe.

She remembered the night before her senior prom, visiting her friends' houses to check out their outfits. She'd been genuinely excited to ooh and aah over Paloma's and Iris's gowns, but once at home, she couldn't help but feel just a teensy bit left out. She hadn't even been asked to the dance. Not even by a freaking *guy*. Her mama, bless her heart, had tried so hard to make things better. She'd cornered Emie's second cousin, Juanito, in the kitchen, and asked him to escort Emie to the festivities since she Couldn't Get A Date. Talk about a booby prize. Emie had never been so mortified, more so when she saw the emotions on Juanito's face move from shock to horror to resignation…to that fucking omnipresent pity. She'd faked cramps to weasel out of the mercy date with her cousin. Never again. Being alone wasn't nearly as bad as being pitied.

In fact, being alone suited her just fine.

Besides, who cared? That was a long time ago, and she had a house to paint. "Let it go," she said, to herself and her friends at the same time. "I'm not looking for a relationship, and I'm not interested in Gia. Let's get going before it gets too hot out here."

Three hours later, with only a tiny section of the front of her house done, Emie, Iris, and Paloma sprawled on lounge chairs sipping iced tea and resting their tired limbs.

"I didn't know this was going to be so damned hard," Emie said. Painting was exhausting, tedious, irritating work. Her arms ached, her calves were cramped, and it seemed like they'd barely made any progress. That was the worst part.

"We need help," Paloma added.

"Screw help. We need to pay someone to finish," said Iris, voicing what they'd all been thinking. "This is hell. This is why sane people hire professionals."

"Oh, shut up," Emie said.

Pep and Teddy glanced up when a big black pickup truck rumbled to the curb, then six-year-old Pep whipped his head around and announced, "Someone's here in a 2004 Ford F350, Auntie Emie."

Emie looked over in time to see Gia's long, muscular, denim-clad legs stretch below the driver's door. When the door slammed, her curvy, V-shaped upper body, looking fine in a fitted tank top, came into view. Emie lurched upright, sloshing iced tea on her paint-spattered overshirt.

Four-year-old Teddy jumped to his feet and bounced across the lawn, stopping at Gia's boots. He leaned his little crew-cut way back, looking up at a smiling Gia, and said, "We don't live here, but my auntie does. Can I sit'n your truck? Is it yours? Who're you?"

"Teodoro!" Paloma called. "Mind your manners."

Gia laughed and ruffled Teddy's head. "I'm a friend of your auntie's. I'm Gia."

Teddy bolted across the lawn hollering, "Auntie Emie, your friend Gia is here in her black Ford Extra Cab four-by-four!" before a caterpillar caught his attention on the sidewalk.

Emie cast a scowling glance at her grinning, paint-polka-dotted friends, and then tried to decide whether to get up and go meet Gia or wait where she sat. Since her legs felt wobbly and weak, she stayed seated and focused on convincing herself that she wasn't excited to see Gia. Not at all. Not one iota. Not.

Gia ambled across the lawn toward them, the sable brown

eyes Emie remembered hidden behind a pair of sunglasses. Gia glanced up at the house and her lip twitched to the side. "Morning, ladies."

"What are you doing here?" Emie asked, immediately chastising herself for her rudeness. "I mean—"

"It's okay. I was in the neighborhood. What's up?"

"They're paintin' the house," Pep told her, not looking up. The boy sat on one leg, and the other folded knee jutted up in front of him, providing a perfect spot for him to rest his chin while he lined up his car collection.

Gia turned to him. "You helping?"

"No way," Pep said, glancing up. "I'm just a kid."

"That's some shiner you've got for a kid." Gia squatted and studied the bluish purple ring around the boy's left eye.

Pep shrugged. "It doesn't hurt anymore."

Gia stood and turned back to the three women. "I'd be glad to help with the painting."

"No, thanks," Emie said, while Paloma and Iris echoed, "That would be great." The women glared at each other before Paloma turned a smile back at Gia.

"It's Emie's house. I guess it's up to her."

Gia looked at Emie, raising one eyebrow.

"We're fine," Emie said. "We can handle it."

"Suit yourself. But I am a painter, you know."

"I don't want a fresco on the front of the damn thing." She sniffed. "I just want a nice coat of Spring Eggshell, and we're perfectly capable of doing that."

"Speak for yourself, Superwoman," Paloma muttered, so her boys couldn't hear. "This shit sucks."

Gia took off her sunglasses and smiled from Paloma to Iris. "I'm Gia Mendez," she told them, leaning forward to shake their hands, which provided Emie a clear view down the woman's tank top that she *should not* have taken. She looked away to hide the hunger she was sure showed in her eyes.

"Paloma Vargas." She gestured at the yard. "Those yard

monkeys out there are my boys, Pep and Teodoro. Say hello, *m'ijos.*"

"Hi," the boys chimed with a decided lack of interest.

"And this is Iris Lujan," Paloma finished.

Gia did a double take at Iris. "Wow. Whoa. Hold up. *The* Iris Lujan?"

Iris shrugged, genuine and unaffected as ever. "That would be me. Paint covered and all."

"It's a pleasure to meet you both." Gia crossed toned arms over her chest and smiled politely at Iris. "My eighteen-year-old niece has magazine pictures of you all over her room. I hope that doesn't creep you out. She'll pass out when I tell her I saw you in person, though."

Surprise filtered through Emie at Gia's words. Gia was thrilled to meet a celebrity, no doubt. But she wasn't ogling Iris, like most people did—men *and* women.

Iris laughed and said, "Nope, not creeped out. Just be sure to stand clear of furniture and other hazards when you tell her. I wouldn't want to be responsible for a cracked skull." She tipped her head and peered down the row of lounge chairs. "That's our rude friend, Emie, over there. But I guess you two have already met."

Emie forced a wan smile. What would she do in this situation if it wasn't Gia standing at the foot of her chaise, casting a cool shadow over her overheated body? Ah, yes. Hospitality. "Can I… get you some iced tea, Gia?"

"I'm good," she replied.

Oh, hell, yeah. Emie didn't doubt that claim for a millisecond.

"I actually came about the apartment you have advertised for rent." She pointed to the sign posted in the front yard.

"It's been rented," Emie blurted, just as Paloma and Iris said, "It's available." They exchanged another set of meaningful glances.

Gia smirked. "I get the drill now. It's Emie's house, we'll leave it up to her."

Emie swallowed past a throat that felt like it was coated with drying Spring Eggshell all-weather paint. "What I mean is, it's not, um, ready to rent yet."

"Then why the sign?" Gia hitched her head back in the general direction of it. The question wasn't accusatory. More... curious.

Paloma scrambled to her feet, followed by Iris. Both of them headed for the house. "Boys, come on. Auntie Iris and I are going to make you lunch."

"We'll wait here," Teddy said in a monotone, mesmerized by the caterpillar inching its way up the front of his T-shirt.

"No, you won't. Come on, Teddy. And leave that caterpillar out here. Pep? Put your cars away. Or leave them there. Whatever works."

Emie sat forward, her heart rattling at the thought of being left alone with Gia. "Paloma, wait—"

Paloma ignored her protests. "Now, little men."

"Aw, Mom!" Pep whined. "It ain't lunchtime—"

"Don't say 'ain't.'"

"It *isn't* lunchtime," he said. "We just ate breakfast. I'll barf."

"Listen to your mo-ther," Iris sang.

Prickly heat clawed up Emie's neck and, out of her peripheral vision, she saw Gia grinning. The woman obviously knew what was up. How excruciating. Damn Iris and Paloma. Emie imagined this was like being unwillingly propelled into a blind date.

Pep continued to protest. Amongst moans and groans, he and Teddy scuffed to their feet and grudgingly followed the two traitorous *brujas* from hell into the house. For a few moments after they left, Emie sat stiffly in her lounge chair and concentrated on the birds chirping in the Japanese maple. Or pretended to, at any rate. *Awkwaaaard.* Soon, Gia stretched out on the chaise next to her with a sigh of satisfaction and the ease of a woman who belonged there.

"Gotta love this Colorado weather," she said.

Emie watched an enormous white thunderhead float across the blue sky and took surreptitious glances at Gia's long legs and familiar black boots. What could she possibly say to this woman that wouldn't come off sounding insane or trite? *I want you? I don't want you? Stay? Go away?* She'd never been more attracted to or more confused by a woman, and she still doubted Gia's motives. But they couldn't just sit here and ignore each other or she'd go mad. Emie took a deep breath. She crossed her arms beneath her breasts and said, "So."

"So."

A stiff pause. "You're here again."

"You doubted I would be?" Gia's words held a smile.

Emie swallowed back her reply. Of course she doubted it. Almost as much as she hoped she'd be wrong. She couldn't start getting all ridiculously mushy. Hell, she didn't even have mushy in her repertoire. "Listen, I'm not a game player, so let's cut to the chase. What do you want from me, Gia?"

She felt Gia's piercing gaze on the side of her face for several long moments. It burned as though those tantalizing fingers had touched her. Instead of answering the question, Gia said, "Your rash is going away."

Emie lifted a hand to her neck and cut a quick peek at Gia. "I thought you were gone. Back to Chicago, or…wherever." She listened to the rapid beating of wings as several spooked birds took flight from the branches of the maple. Her stomach felt like the birds' wings were beating against its walls as she waited for Gia's response. She tried to focus on the matter at hand and fought not to let Gia's soapy, just-showered female freshness distract her. When she couldn't stand the suspense anymore, she turned and found those liquid brown eyes staring at her.

"Why won't you rent me your apartment, Emie?"

Gia's smooth voice cooled her and heated her simultaneously.

Everything about this woman was distracting and attracting, every word she spoke made Emie want to touch her. And more. Which simply wasn't her M.O. If she didn't stay aloof around Gia, she'd wind up in a world of hurt. "Because I don't know why you want it."

Gia chuckled and ran those hands through her long, slick hair. "Well, for one, staying in a hotel is costly."

"There are a lot of apartments in the Denver area. The housing market is wide open."

"And for two, you're the only person in Denver I know."

"You don't know me."

"I'd like to change that. That's reason number three."

Emie shook her head slowly, unable to hold back her mirthless laugh. "Okay, okay. Jesus. I forgive you for the show. Is that what you want to hear? Will that make you stop trying so hard to work out your guilt? I forgive you," she enunciated sharply. "You are free to leave."

For several moments, nothing. Then, "Has it ever occurred to you, Emie, that perhaps I just like being around you?"

Her tummy clenched. "Ah, no. I'm not that naïve. I remember how our paths crossed. Surely you haven't forgotten, either."

"Oh, no. I remember." Gia expelled a sigh. "Let me ask you this. In the makeup room, before…"

Emie sensed Gia's discomfort and, for a moment, felt bad for her.

"Did you enjoy talking to me?"

"Sure, but that was before I realized you were just blowing sunshine up my ass."

"Emie, don't," Gia chastised softly. She reached out, settling one soft hand on Emie's leg. Gently. Innocently.

Emie stared down at the exquisite fingers with which Gia had touched her, willing them to stay but knowing she should tell Gia to remove them. But she said nothing. Probably didn't even draw a breath. And then Gia started caressing her leg in small, promising circles, and Emie's world rocked.

"You and I both know we hit it off in that room, *querida.* Despite everything. You were beautiful then, and you're beautiful now. With or without makeup, Emie Jaramillo, you make my mind work and my heart pound. But that isn't what matters."

Emie blinked at Gia, then poked her glasses up.

"Even though you're beautiful, I couldn't care less what you look like on the outside, because you're one of those women who's beautiful on the inside, and it shows." Gia's mouth twisted to the side, and her voice went huskier. "Why can't you believe me?"

Did Emie dare trust the intoxicating words of this woman? She wanted to. But she couldn't bear to set herself up for more pain. Her skin tingled from head to foot, and when she darted her tongue out to moisten her parched lips, she saw Gia's gaze drop to her mouth and deepen. Desire pooled low within her, a steady, wet throb that wouldn't stop. God, she didn't want it to stop. "First of all, I couldn't give a rat's ass if I meet society's beauty standards, so let's lay that on the table once and for all."

"Done."

"And the other point…I won't be your pity project, Gia. Not now, not ever."

"You never would be."

"I'm not looking for a relationship. My career is my life. I'm not some desperate…single—" she sputtered, though it felt like someone knifed her heart when she said the words.

"I didn't come here to hook up with you, Emie. I mean, not necessarily. We can just be friends if that's what you want." Gia's hand slid from her leg. "I'm cool with that." A beat passed. "Is that what you want?"

"I…I guess." *No. I don't know.* Emie sighed and turned her head away, gathering her wits, gauging Gia's motives. What would it hurt to be friends? As long as the boundaries were clear, and they both respected them, things wouldn't get out of control. She needed a renter, Gia needed a place to live. Emie was perfectly capable of resisting the indisputable sexual draw. Gia was just a woman, for God's sake. *A sinuous stretch of kissable, toned, bronze female flesh, that is.* Emie nudged her glasses down, closed her eyes, and pinched the bridge of her nose. What was she—love-struck? Sixteen and stupid? No matter what the woman looked like or how sweetly she talked, Emie could manage a platonic relationship with Gia Mendez, makeup artist and painter. She *could.*

Wait a minute. Her eyes popped open.

With a rush of anticipation, she realized Gia possessed talents she obviously didn't. Skills and know-how that could help her regain her pride. Gia wouldn't dare refuse her, even if she didn't agree with the plan. Emie would play on Gia's guilt if she had to. And—facts were facts—this brainstorm would meet both their needs.

"There's good light in the carriage house apartment," she murmured, clearing her throat. "I mean, for your painting. I can give you a couple months rent free so you can get on your feet if—"

"Hold up." Hope lit up Gia's eyes, pulled the corner of her mouth into a half smile. "Does that mean—?"

"Yes," Emie said. "It's yours, but only on a couple of conditions."

Gia crossed her arms, bare biceps flexing. "Name them."

Emie angled her head toward their slapdash paint job and rolled her eyes. "One, you finish painting this damned house."

Gia laughed. "I knew you'd come around on that issue. No problem there."

"Two, we both understand that we're friends." She fixed her future tenant with her most earnest stare. "Just friends. I'm not looking for…entanglements." *Pity entanglements—no thanks.*

Gia shrugged one shoulder. "I'll admit, that rule's a drag, but if that's how it has to be, okay. We've got a deal."

"Not so fast. One other thing." Emie's morning coffee burned in her gut. She splayed a palm over her torso and pressed.

Gia urged her on with a nod.

"I want you..." She faltered, afraid to utter the words, afraid the idea was insane. Afraid. Her teeth cut into her bottom lip for a moment.

"Just say it."

"I want you to help me change my image. Makeup, hair, all of it. You're a professional, and that's what I need."

Gia looked baffled. "But why? You look great."

No. Emie wouldn't fall for that line again. "My reasons are my reasons. Besides, I don't want to look like this anymore. I don't want to be remembered for that show."

"If that's what you want, okay." A small line bisected Gia's brows. "But what exactly do you hope to achieve with this... makeover?"

Turning toward her, Emie hiked up her chin just daring Gia to scoff at her. Taking one more deep breath for courage, she said, "I want to look sexy, like a bombshell. I want you to make me irresistible to Vitoria Elizalde."

CHAPTER FOUR

Gia could understand Emie's need to regain control, to make some changes in her appearance in order to recover from the blow dealt by *The Barry Stillman Show*. A lot of people changed some aspect of their looks after a major stressor. What she couldn't quite grasp was Emie's desire to become irresistible to a pompous, mean-spirited player when here Gia sat, next to her, ready, willing, and thinking she was fifty kinds of irresistible already. Women. Who could figure them out?

She studied Emie. Tension buzzed just beneath her surface, even though her casual posture belied the fact. Stretched out on the adjacent lounge chair, slim and tentative as a gazelle, a passerby would likely peg her as relaxed. Gia knew better. Emie was waiting for an answer. Sunlight shone on the locks of hair that peeked out of the front of Emie's backwards baseball cap, and a dollop of paint had dried right on the tip of her straight, kissable nose. Even dressed in an oversized, paint-splattered men's shirt and cut-offs, Emie looked every inch the brilliant scientist Gia knew her to be.

And then it hit her.

Perhaps Emie wanted that sharp-eyed Elizalde bitch because they were of the same intellectual level. Maybe Gia's own questionable charms had no effect on Emie because she didn't measure up where it counted in Emie's world. Gia was, after all, nothing more than a starving artist, a woman with simple needs. She couldn't possibly stimulate Emie's exquisite brain, and just possibly the educated snake could. The thought made Gia clench her jaw until her teeth ground.

Elizalde didn't deserve Emie.

Maybe you don't deserve her either, G. You hurt her. A sting of sadness hit her like a gut punch. Who was she trying to kid? Facts were sobering facts: Emie didn't want her because of what had happened on *The Stillman Show*. In the first few moments she'd known Emie, she'd betrayed her, and some things, once done, couldn't be undone. She would do everything in her power to make up for that, even if it meant setting aside her misplaced desire for Emie, at least for the time being. Even if it meant giving a makeover to a woman who didn't need one. No sense trying to sweet-talk the doc, because Emie wasn't having it. She still thought Gia had come to Denver out of a sense of pity.

"Well?" Emie blinked from behind her glasses. "Will you agree to all the conditions?"

Uh, yeah. Mama didn't raise no fool. She'd go along with anything if it meant spending time with Emie, even this absurd makeover idea. If Gia had her own agenda in the whole jacked-up plan, well, Emie didn't need to know it. This would give Gia time to redeem herself, and after that, she'd show the lovely Dr. Jaramillo she could arouse her brain as well as her senses, no matter their educational differences. But for now, she wouldn't come on too strong. Throwing the full Mendez Mack Action at this point would just scare Emie away. Gia would let Emie take the lead and, with any luck, she'd come around.

"Of course I'll do it. It would be my pleasure to be of service to you." Emie wanted bombshell? Gia would lay it on thick. So thick, in fact, Emie would realize her mistake and put a stop to the whole thing. It'd work. It *had* to work.

"Then it's a deal, thank you." Emie's tone softened. "I really appreciate this." She laid her delicate hand on Gia's arm and squeezed. For a moment Gia's mind reeled. This kind of gratitude, she could get used to. She'd work on giving Emie better reasons to touch her body with those velvety hands, but for now, the thank-you worked well enough.

"*You* appreciate it?" Gia chuckled. "You're saving me from a road trip to nowhere."

A wrinkle of worry touched Emie's forehead, and her fingers moved to her bottom lip. "I didn't even stop to consider your situation. I just assumed…can you stay in Denver?"

Mr. Fuentes always told her, if you don't have anywhere to go, you better start liking where you are. Gia spread her arms and grinned. "I'm all yours. Two months' free rent might be just the jump-start my art career needs." *And it will give me time to show you I'm the woman you need.* She relaxed back, feeling better than she had in a long time.

"What are you going to do to me first?" Emie asked.

A dagger of desire impaled Gia, and for a moment she couldn't breathe. Emie's gaze was clear, her question innocent of innuendo, but Gia was damn proud to be a red-blooded Latina lesbian. It took every ounce of restraint not to leap on the double entendre she read into Emie's words.

Damn.

Was she the only one feeling this undercurrent of electricity between them?

Against her natural inclinations, she adopted an all-business attitude. "First off, I need to get moved in. Next, I finish painting the house. Then"—she clapped her palms together, then rubbed them slowly as she fully assessed Emie—"how much time do we have?"

"The fall faculty get-together is on August sixth, so about"—Emie's eyes shifted up and to the left as she calculated—"four weeks." Doubt clouded her expression. "Can we pull it off?"

"That's more than enough time. We'll do your hair first."

Emie tucked her chin like a puppy used to getting smacked. "Okay."

Gia narrowed her gaze. Perhaps she should be extra gentle

with Emie's feelings; she couldn't quite read her yet, but no harm in erring on the side of caution. "Not that your hair needs work. It's just, we have to start somewhere."

"No worries," Emie said, reaching up to toy with what little hair stuck out from beneath her cap. "Frankly, I could use the help. I aimed for Halle Barry and somehow wound up with third-grade boy."

"I wouldn't go that far." Gia laughed, then couldn't help herself from testing the boundaries. She lowered her tone into a velvet caress. "I figure I'll just start at your head and make my way slowly down your body until I have it all covered. Sound good?" A sly grin begged to make an appearance, but she held it back. She watched Emie holding her breath and knew she was staving off those endearing hiccups.

Finally, Emie found her voice, breathy and feminine. "Uh... it, um, yes. Sounds good."

Gia definitely wore those cute cheeky shorts, Emie decided. Or maybe nothing. Or maybe she shouldn't be gawking at Gia's backside with unabashed lust, but, damn, she just couldn't help it. She stared dry-mouthed at the skin-exposing rip in Gia's jeans—just below her perfectly curved ass—as Gia descended the ladder to retrieve the ice water Emie'd brought out. When Gia's foot reached the bottom rung, Emie tore her reverence from that toned, sun-gleaming body and focused on the fresh coat of Spring Eggshell paint on her house. Her mind's eye remained firmly on Gia's ass, though. "God, it looks *so* good."

Gia turned to her, a curious smile on her face. She studied Emie over the rim of the glass as she took a long draw of water, then wiped the back of her hand slowly across her lips. "Such glowing admiration could make a painter wish she were the paint job itself."

"Ha ha," Emie replied in a tart but playful tone. *If she only knew.* Emie shifted her gaze to the ground, but not before it had swept down Gia's bare, toned, sweat-sheened and paint-spattered arms. She noted the unfastened top button of Gia's jeans with unabashed interest. "I really appreciate you getting this all buttoned up. Finished, I mean."

"No sweat. Well, lots of sweat. But it's calming work," Gia said. "Gives me time to think about my current project."

With dismay, Emie realized she'd been so focused on her own issues lately, she hadn't even bothered to inquire about Gia and her life. Her artwork, for God's sake. "How's that going? Are you all settled in?"

Gia nodded. "After I finish the new painting, I think I may take a few pieces around to some of the galleries in town, see what kind of response I get."

"That's a wonderful idea. I'd love to see your work," she hinted, hoping Gia'd offer to take a break and show her right that freaking minute. She supposed she could learn a lot about the woman that way.

"Sometime, sure," Gia said, but sounded unconvincing.

Gulp. Emie felt the conversation dwindling to a close and racked her brain for something to revive it. "What's the new painting? Can I take a peek at that one?"

Gia hiked up one shoulder, her gaze distant, as though looking inward rather than out. "I never show my works-in-progress until they're no longer in progress." Gia plucked an ice cube from the glass and ran it over the back of her neck and upper chest. A low sound of satisfaction rumbled from her throat, making Emie's lungs tighten. "I needed this," she said. "It's hot today."

Speak, Em. Say something. She'd guided technical lectures, spoken before grant review boards with eloquence and grace, yet nothing intelligent came to mind when presented with such brazen feminine appeal. Well, that certainly knocked one job off her list of alternate careers. She could never work as an announcer in a women's strip club. She'd be tongue-tied the whole time. "August," she blurted.

Gia blinked. "I'm sorry?"

"August is usually Colorado's hottest month," Emie said, crossing her arms over her torso. "You haven't seen the worst of the heat wave yet." *Weather. Yes. Innocuous and socially acceptable. Let's talk about that.* She didn't want to ponder the image of Gia running that dripping ice cube over *her* naked skin.

Yes. She. Did.

Emie was the one to insist they keep things platonic, so why did she want to kick herself for that rule every time she saw the woman? Over these first three days of Gia's residence in the carriage house, they'd fallen into an easy, polite friendship. They met on the back porch each morning and shared coffee and sections of *The Denver Post.* Gia had kept up her half of the deal by being nothing but a gentlewoman. Almost—ugh, dared she say it? Sisterly. Yet here Emie stood lusting after the woman like a cat in heat and wishing her feelings were reciprocated. How fickle could she be?

She had probably concocted fifty weak excuses to come outside and gape while Gia painted her house, wearing only ripped jeans and a barely there tank top. Jesus, Emie had to pull herself together.

"But it's a dry heat, yeah?" Gia grinned.

"What? Oh. Yes." Emie pushed her lips into the semblance of a normal smile and watched Gia's throat move as she drained the glass. A rivulet of melting ice trickled slowly down the contours of Gia's chest, into that sacred, fragrant place between her breasts, and her nipples hardened beneath the threadbare white tank.

Dios mío, call the fire department.

"What are your plans tonight?" Gia asked, extending the empty glass toward her.

Emie jerked her gaze to the other woman's face, then took

the tumbler, clutching it to her chest. She hoped to hide her own hardened nipples, hardened for a whole other reason besides ice. "Uh, I don't have any. I was going to peruse some lab studies, but they aren't pressing. Why?"

Gia squinted up at the house, then stooped to gather some painting supplies into a neat pile on the sidewalk. "I thought we'd discuss some options for the makeover…over dinner, wherever you'd like," she said casually. "Then we could catch some live jazz at El Chapultepec." She stood, hands on hips.

Emie's lips parted. Was Gia inviting her out?

As if reading Emie's thoughts, Gia raised her palms. "Before you protest, I assure you, it'll just be two friends grabbing a bite and checking out music."

"I-I know." Irrational disappointment fizzled through Emie. "My treat."

"Oh. Well. I'm perfectly capable of paying my own way."

"Whatever you'd like."

Nothing seemed to faze the woman. She pulled the elastic from her ponytail and furrowed paint-flecked fingers through that gorgeous swing of hair. Sweat dampened her hairline, the back of her neck.

"I've heard a lot about El Chapultepec's world-class jazz. It'll be more enjoyable together."

What wouldn't be more enjoyable alongside Gia? Emie thought. She'd never even heard of El Chapultepec, such was the extent of her dismal nightlife experience. Even so, her heart quickened at the thought of an evening out with Gia. It wasn't a date, but it kind of felt like one. The ridiculous urge to spin in a circle ribboned through her. She was *such* a dork. "I've never been there. But that would be fine," she stammered. "Not fine. Fun, actually. So, yes. When should we go?"

The low-hanging afternoon sun burnished Gia's face in warm gold light, highlighting her high cheekbones and effortless, endless beauty. She smiled, looking genuinely pleased. "Really?

Great. I need to straighten up here, then grab a shower. Let's say, an hour? Will that give you enough time?"

Emie nodded, firm and businesslike. "See you then. I'll bring a notebook and pen."

"A notebook and—why?" Confusion clouded Gia's eyes.

"So we can take notes, write down our plan." Emie adjusted her glasses, her skin heating with embarrassment instantly. But why? "For the makeover. You said we'd discuss it over dinner. That's the whole point, right?" *Please say no.*

"Oh. Right. Of course." The corners of Gia's full mouth quivered. "Good, uh, you bring those things. That'll save me the trouble of digging 'em up myself." The diamond stud in her earlobe caught the sunlight.

Emie turned and took hesitant steps toward the porch, wondering about the look of amusement on Gia's face. She felt like she'd made some kind of social blunder but had no clue what it was and didn't have time to dwell on it. She only had an hour to get ready. Ugh. Dread. She didn't *date.* By choice. She didn't have a damn clue how this whole thing would go down. She slowed and finally turned back, cheeks burning. "Gia? I'm sorry. What do you suppose I should wear…to such a place?" She bit the corner of her lip as humiliation bubbled up inside her for having to show how woefully inept she was at this type of social engagement.

Gia closed the space between them in seconds and touched her nose with one paint-coated finger. "Whatever you choose will look perfect, *querida.* It's not a fancy spot by any means. Wear whatever makes you comfortable."

Emie released a pent-up breath. A smile lifted her lips, and her skin tingled where Gia had brushed it. Sadly, it was a new sensation being touched by a woman, and Emie—not so surprisingly—enjoyed the attention. "Thank you," she said, and meant it. Gia Mendez was a nice woman. She made Emie feel less like a freakish scientist and more like the vibrant, vital woman she'd shelved decades earlier. After the Barry Stillman debacle, she never thought she'd admit it, but she was glad Gia had come to Denver.

❖

The famous jazz club was nothing more than a minuscule hole in the wall on the corner of Twentieth and Blake in lower downtown. Emie crossed the threshold, welcomed by a doorwoman who smiled but didn't check their IDs. The place seemed pretty full for a weeknight, men and women nursing beverages and bouncing their heads gently to the beat of the music. The black summer wool slacks and cherry red silk blouse Emie had chosen were on the conservative side, but she didn't feel the least bit self-conscious. Gia had told her she looked wonderful; that was enough to bolster her.

The back room was a brashly lit cantina offering no-nonsense food and a pool table. They'd just finished a meal at the restaurant next door, though, so they scanned the bar area close to the musicians. They spied a couple vacating a wood and vinyl booth halfway between the door and the tiny stage and made a beeline for it. Emie slid in, surprised that Gia took the seat beside her instead of across the table. Emie raised a quizzical brow.

"You mind? I'm a visual person. I like to be able to watch the musicians." Gia propped the heels of her boots on the bench across from them and settled in.

"I don't mind." Was Gia nuts? Sitting next to her was a treat. Emie let her eyes wander around the darkened interior. Photographs of musicians who'd played there lined the walls, frame to frame. Pink bar lights shone off the black and white floor tiles and glinted off the chrome edges of the Formica tables. Up front, four musicians crowded a small, battered stage, filling the club with music through a surprisingly good-quality sound system. ONE DRINK MINIMUM PER SET, a large sign near the stage stated.

An attractive young waitress dressed in jeans and a green

tank top approached the table. She spared Emie a minor glance before her ravenous gaze and 300-watt smile rested comfortably on Gia. "Well, how are you this evening?" Her voice held a whiskey rasp served up with a side shot of confident sexuality. "What can I bring you?"

Gia turned from the waitress to her. "Emie?"

"Whatever you're having," she said, catching the waitress's "notice me" posture out of the corner of her eye.

Gia ordered them each a coffee with Frangelico as Emie lost herself in the husky tunes, ignoring the waitress's blatant flirting with Gia. The chick might as well have straddled Gia's lap to take the order. How irksome. What was Emie, invisible? Sure, she didn't have any hold over Gia, but how would the waitress know that? Was it so obvious that a woman like Emie would never truly be with someone extraordinary like Gia?

Her stomach cramped. *Don't think about it. You have more brain power in your little finger than that bitch has at all.*

When their coffees came, Emie glanced over and realized with a start how close the two of them sat. Gia's body heat pulled her in like a magnetic force field. If she turned her head, she could probably count the barely perceptible freckles dusting Gia's bronzed cheeks. Gia's arm draped casually over the back of the booth, long fingers tapping out the beat next to Emie's head. This proximity set her senses dancing, and despite the irrationality of it, she yearned to edge even nearer, to nestle into Gia's warm sugar scent. She closed her eyes and allowed herself to fantasize how it would feel for Gia Mendez to actually be attracted to her. For her to actually let a woman break through that impenetrable emotional wall she'd built so long ago. One song ended, and another began.

"It's just my opinion," Gia said next to her ear, that hot, creamy voice vibrating against Emie's skin until she could hardly bear it, "but there's just something blatantly erotic about saxophone music. Yeah?"

Emie swallowed with effort, her lids fluttering open. A simple question. She didn't know about the music itself, but there was definitely something erotic about a lethally sexy woman breathing on your neck in a hot smoky jazz club while saxophone rhythms thumped their way into your soul. *That* she could, surprisingly enough, get used to. She brushed her hand against the side of her neck. "Yes. It's…it's lovely," she finally managed.

Gia's soft laughter brought Emie's gaze to her profile. She tried to look indignant, though the coffee and companionship had mellowed her into a great mood. "Are you laughing at me?"

"I'm laughing *with* you, Emie." Gia squeezed her shoulder.

Emie crossed her arms and raised an eyebrow. "Well, considering the fact that I'm not laughing, what's so funny?"

Gia shifted to face her so she didn't have to speak into Emie's ear to be heard over the sultry bass pumping through the packed crowd, through their conversation, through their bodies. Pink light caught one side of her face while shadows claimed the other. "I don't know…you make me happy."

"How so?"

"Here I am talking about sax music being erotic, sensual, and you say it's lovely." Gia shrugged. "You're different from the other women I've known. You're just so…real."

Inside, Emie warmed. But she arched a brow. "You thought I was an illusion?"

Gia danced soft fingers along Emie's shoulder, studying her face with an intensity Emie could hardly bear. "Sometimes I wonder."

Deprived of a reply, Emie turned her attention back to the band, feeling light and tingly and alive. Pulsating. Sexual. Gia said the nicest things to her, all the time. One would almost think Gia found her awkwardness attractive. Right then, it didn't matter if Gia was schmoozing, trying to charm her way into Emie's good graces to make up for what had happened. The flattery soothed like a balm, and Emie just wanted to enjoy the company for a while. Gia was witty and attentive, and oh so gorgeous. Emie felt warm and special tucked next to her in the booth, even if it wasn't a "real" date.

Her mind wandered to their earlier discussion about the makeover. They'd shoot for an exotic look, Gia had suggested over a dinner of West Texas burgers and home fries. Elizalde hailed from Brazil, she'd explained, and many Brazilian women went for that style. For Emie, "exotic" brought to mind fruit basket hats and fuchsia feather boas, but she was sure it meant something else altogether to Gia. She certainly hoped so, anyway.

She leaned closer. "Do me a favor. If you see a woman who has this exotic look we're trying for, point her out."

"Gladly." Gia immediately scanned the crowd.

Emie tried to follow her gaze, but found herself staring at the sweep of Gia's strong yet feminine jawline instead, yearning to touch it. Even masked by the enticing scents of chile and fresh baked tortillas wafting in from the kitchen, Gia smelled soapy fresh and audaciously, edibly womanly. Emie didn't think Gia wore cologne, but that was the point. She didn't need any help smelling incredible.

"There's an exotic-looking woman." Gia inclined her head toward a table adjacent to the stage.

Emie tracked her line of sight until she caught a glimpse of the woman in question, and her stomach plunged, though not nearly as far as the woman's neckline. Wait. Maybe she was looking at the wrong person. Emie scanned the booths, but besides Ms. Cleavage, only men occupied the seats. From her poofed-up hair to her garish makeup and painted-on clothes, the woman looked nothing like what Emie had pictured as exotic. She looked like a…a total slut. A *straight* slut.

"You can't possibly mean her?" Emie balked, resisting the urge to laugh out loud. "In the purple minidress?"

Gia smiled with what could only be interpreted as sloe-eyed approval. "That's her. Looks great, yeah?"

Emie's hand fluttered to her throat, her eyes fixed on the overblown caricature of the stereotypical barfly. Was this the kind of woman who turned Gia's head? A little coil of disappointed jealousy sprang free inside her. She could never carry off that look, not that she had any desire to do so. She took a large swallow of her coffee and reminded herself she wasn't trying to interest Gia. She wasn't. The whole point of this was to get back at Vitoria.

Period.

"Well, I guess you could say she looks…exotic." Emie fiddled with her coffee mug. "A bit much, though, don't you think?"

"Are you kidding? If anything, she's a little tame."

"Tame?" Dread surged through her. "No way. She looks—"

"*¿Qué?*"

Nose scrunched, she tipped her head side to side, searching for a kinder phrase, before giving in and saying what had immediately come to her mind. "She looks…paid for."

Gia laughed, leaning her head back. "You won't look exactly like that, don't worry. By exotic, I just mean a style."

"But *that* style?"

"We're talking about a wealthy, worldly Brazilian scientist," Gia reminded her. "Vitoria could have her pick of women. We have to choose a look that stands out from the crowd."

Emie's throat closed at the prospect of standing out in that manner. She'd look like the poster child for cheap and desperate cougars. Then again, what did she know? Gia had her finger on the pulse of fashion. Emie would have to trust her judgment about what would attract other women.

"She certainly does…stand out, I guess." Her dubious gaze fell to the woman's neckline again. She'd never fill a dress like that. They only had four weeks, and short of plastic surgery, her pert breasts were doomed to remain virtually cleavage-free. "Miracle Bra" was just a brand name, after all.

"This is what you wanted, right, *querida*?" Gia's tone lowered as the musicians ended one song to a smattering of enthusiastic applause. "To look different from how you do right now? To attract Elizalde? 'Make me a bombshell,' I think you said."

Emie's head nodded as her mind screamed, "No!" She pushed her drink farther away, unsure if she had the stomach for finishing it. "I do want that, but…maybe purple minidress woman is a bad example. Find someone else who falls into the exotic realm."

Gia glanced around, finally pointing at an in-your-face blonde wearing a royal blue leather bustier and matching miniskirt. "She has the style."

Emie gaped, nauseated. She couldn't even feign approval of the blonde's immodest outfit. Mama would have a stroke if she saw Emie wearing that. She'd have a stroke *herself*. "Uh…okay. Anyone else?"

"In the hot pink." Gia pointed. "Over there."

Three strikes, and I'm out, thought Emie, catching sight of the bottle redhead Gia had indicated. If these examples were any indication of her fashion future, she was doomed to look trashy. Not that she begrudged the three women their personal choices, but the look just wasn't *her*. Yet that was how Gia envisioned her metamorphosis? What a horrifying mistake she'd made with this stupid revenge idea.

Dismay settled like wet leaves in her stomach, and she directed her attention to the street outside the window. She'd instigated the whole plan, so she couldn't back out now. For all she knew, it would work. Perhaps the core of her beauty problem resided in her fear of taking risks. Wearing skintight blue leather might actually exhilarate and empower her, who knew? She sincerely doubted it, but, if Gia thought it would work…

"I've told you already," Gia said, as though reading her mind, "you don't need to change. If you want to go through with this, that's fine. If not, that's okay, too. Not that my opinion counts for much after, well, everything. But you're perfect as you are."

"Is that why I ended up on *The Barry Stillman Show*?"

Gia maintained a calm expression, but Emie noticed her fists clench. "You ended up on the show because Elizalde is a no-good, deceitful—"

"Don't worry. I'll take care of the good professor." She flicked the words away as though swatting a bug. "As for this makeover, you don't have to coddle me, Gia. I'm a grown woman. I know I need work."

"We'll have to agree to disagree on that point." She covered Emie's hand with her own, then quickly released it. "But I've already told you I'd make you over. Your wish is my command. So, tell me what you want."

A morose sigh escaped her lips. "I know it's shallow and irrelevant, not to mention completely lame and out of character for me. But I just want to feel...gorgeous. Just this once." Emie wasn't sure if it was the liqueur or the way Gia's eyes darkened as she stared at her, but liquid warmth surged through her, rendering her limbs buoyant and weightless. When Gia looked at her, she *really* looked at her. As if she mattered more than anyone else. She'd never experienced anything like it.

"Don't you worry, *querida*," Gia said finally, her words a caress. "I've got all kinds of ways to make you feel like the most gorgeous woman in the world."

Emie wanted to believe her. She really, really did.

CHAPTER FIVE

*P**urple?"*
    "Yes!"

"Gia actually said she was going to dye your hair purple, and you just batted your baby browns and said okay? *¿Estás loca?"* Iris's disbelieving rasp carried across the phone line.

Emie twisted around to scowl out the window toward the carriage house. "No, I'm not crazy, and I didn't bat my eyes. I'm not an eye batter—you know that. I just didn't know how to respond. I seem to have trouble formulating intelligent sentences when I'm around her."

Iris groaned. "You're driving *me* crazy, girl. Just take a breath, back up, and tell me exactly what she said."

Emie tucked the phone between her cheek and shoulder and began emptying the dishwasher to keep her nervous hands occupied. A week had passed since Gia had pointed out the three exotic musketeers at El Chapultepec. It had cracked her resolve to the point that Emie had put her off for several days. But yesterday, Gia had tripped her up. She'd flashed that dimple at her, called her *querida*, and asked when they'd get the show on the road.

"How about tomorrow morning?" Emie had blurted, eager to spend time with Gia. Stupid, stupid. Now, tomorrow was today and there was no turning back.

"She didn't say purple exactly. She said eggplant, which is worse. Eggplant, for God's sake. I just don't know if I can go through with something that drastic, Iris." She hurled a meat fork into the drawer. "I'll look like some emo teenager. I just know it."

"Oh." Iris blew out a breath, and her tone softened. "That's different. That's a pretty popular hair color, Em. It doesn't come out looking purple at all, especially on dark hair like yours and mine. It's pretty. Eggplant's just the name, you know? Is she there yet?"

Emie peered out the window, scanning the carriage house for signs of life. "Would we be having this conversation if she was?"

"Good point."

Emie settled back against the edge of the sink and hung her head, still unsure about dying her hair the color of a bulbous vegetable that, let's be real, very few people liked unless it was deep-fried and doused in sauce. "You're sure it'll be okay?"

"Tell her to do demi-permanent instead of permanent if you're really worried. I think it'll be fine." Iris hesitated. "Listen, Em, I've been meaning to talk to you about this whole thing."

"What's up?"

Iris sighed. "If you're making changes that'll erase the whole Barry Stillman thing from your mind, if you're doing it for you, that's one thing. But if this is part of your ridiculous revenge plan—"

"Ah, sorry to interrupt, but Gia's here, hon," Emie lied, not up for another lecture. Her friends seemed to believe she should just throw herself into Gia's arms and forget about Elizalde. As if *that* would bring her dignity back. As if it were even an option—please. "I'll call you later."

"But, Em—"

Emie cradled the telephone handset gently, then peered back at the carriage house again. Where was she? Anticipation bubbled inside her like an unstable volcano. Despite reservations about her impending dye job, Emie couldn't wait to spend some time with Gia. Though they'd met on the back porch for coffee each morning as usual, Gia had spent the majority of her days in the carriage house working furiously on this new secret project. Emie'd glimpsed her through the large north-facing window several times, which made her feel like a voyeur. But it wasn't her fault the window over her kitchen sink faced Gia's place.

She'd just set the pot of coffee to brew and laid out some crumb cake when Gia darkened the open back door. "Hey-yo, it's not the Avon Lady calling," she said through the screen, punctuating her playful words with a grin.

"Then it must be the L'Oreal woman, because obviously I'm worth it."

"Funny," she replied. "Can you grab the door?"

Emie smoothed her hands down the front of her low-slung jeans as excitement twined with anxiety inside her. She crossed the room and pushed open the squeaky screen door, welcoming Gia with a nervous smile. "C-come on in."

Faded jeans that almost matched hers hugged Gia's toned thighs, and a black T-shirt molded to the sculpted shape of her chest and shoulders. Soft and curvy. Ripped and strong. The ultimate sexy dichotomy. Gia's hair hung damp and loose, and that signature just-showered freshness assailed Emie's senses and filled the room. Gia smelled so familiar, so alive and vibrant, it made Emie dizzy.

"You sound out of breath," Gia said, carting in a plastic cape and what looked like a fishing tackle box.

"I'm, uh, fine." Emie eyed the tools with barely masked concern, then wrapped her arms across her torso and shivered. "Okay, I just lied. I'm nervous as hell."

"*¿Por qué?*" Gia set her things on the wooden dinette and turned back to her, planting her fists on her hips. Her eyes narrowed, and a playful smile tugged that delicious dimple into her smooth cheek. "Still worried I'm gonna give you fluorescent hair?"

Emie blurted a nervous little heh-heh-heh and moved to the cabinet, snagging two mugs off the top shelf. The crisp, welcoming scent of coffee filled the air between them. "You know you're a dead woman if you do. If anything, you should be shaking in those black boots of yours. Eat some coffee cake." She pointed toward it.

"I won't do anything out of control, I promise." She picked up a square of the cake and bit into it. "Mmm, it's hot."

"That's usually how things come out of the oven," Emie teased. "I just made it."

"You made it?" Gia exclaimed, shaking her head, laughter in her eyes. "Smart, beautiful, funny, and she cooks, too. You're a catch, *Profé*. No lie."

"Uh-huh. Sure." Emie didn't believe a word of it, but the words still soothed her. She grabbed a piece of cake and took a nibble, setting the rest on a small plate.

"You know, I started to think you'd changed your mind about this makeover." Gia popped the rest of the breakfast cake into her mouth, then brushed cinnamon-coated fingers together while she chewed and swallowed.

"Not at all. I'm anxious for it. I've just been busy getting ready for the semester." Emie turned away to hide the lie and busied herself pouring their drinks. She didn't have much preparation left for the fall term because, true to form, she'd gotten it all done in the first couple weeks of her break. Being a Type-A personality came in handy now and then.

Without warning, Gia moved behind her and furrowed long, warm fingers into Emie's hair, moving slowly from her nape up along the sides of her head. Emie could feel the heat of Gia's body behind her. Her heart lunged, her breath caught. Goose bumps trailed down her back. Gia's touch sizzled but Emie froze, only remembering to exhale when the steaming brew spilled over the rim of the mug she'd been filling and spread in a pool on the countertop.

"Whoops! I…oh, damnit." She set down the carafe with a sharp clunk and spun to face Gia. Too close. She saw flecks of gold she hadn't noticed before in Gia's brown eyes, noted with dismay that Gia had moistened those soft, full lips of hers with a flick of her tongue. "W-what are you doing?"

Gia blinked innocently, though her expression looked as lust drunk as Emie felt. "Just checking the length of your hair, deciding whether I should trim before I color. I didn't mean to startle you." She rested her palms on the edge of the counter on either side of Emie, boxing her in. Gia's expression turned devious, and she raised her brows. "What did you think I was going to do?" she asked, voice husky. "Kiss you?"

"Well…I…no—" Mortified, Emie poked her glasses up and tried to keep herself from trembling. Her chin raised, and she used her most professorial tone. "Of course not."

"That's good, because we have our agreement and all. Just friends," Gia drawled. Her eyes drank in Emie's face, settling just long enough to be uncomfortable on her mouth. "You remember the rules, *querida*, yeah?"

It took everything within Emie not to bite her lip. Or Gia's. But she had her pride to consider. "Of course, I remember. I made the"—*stupid, short-sighted, infuriating*—"rules."

Gia cocked her head to the side, a rueful half-smile on her lips. "No arguing there." Her gaze dropped to Emie's throat, and her nostrils flared as she inhaled.

Next to the women, coffee ran off the countertop in a trickle, splashing wide on the linoleum. Emie noted it distractedly, then half whispered, "Excuse me." She pointed toward the sink. "I need the dish cloth." Fuck the dish cloth. She needed to get away so every breath she pulled into her lungs wasn't filled with the sugared woman scent of Gia, the promise of her.

The empty promise.

Gia pushed away as if nothing sensual had happened and walked backward until the table stopped her. Stuffing her hands in her back pockets, she just watched.

With as much nonchalance as she could muster, Emie snagged the dish cloth and sopped up the mess on the counter before squatting to swipe at the floor. The air fairly crackled with unspoken tension. The low throb in Emie's body was the very best kind of painful. Unbearable bliss. Long-ignored need. Was she the only one who felt the electricity between them?

She managed stammering small talk while she poured them coffee. It wasn't until she was seated on a bar stool wrapped in Gia's plastic cape that her flustered state had eased enough to facilitate normal conversation.

"I have an appointment to get contact lenses on Monday," she said as Gia combed through her short hair. She clutched her glasses in her lap, the room before her a soft myopic blur. "Maybe we can go shopping for cosmetics some time after that."

"Sure." Gia set the comb down and stepped around in front of her. "No rush. Get used to your contacts first. Your skin is sensitive. I won't be surprised if your eyes are, too."

"Okay." Emie squinted, watching Gia mix some vile-smelling concoction in a small plastic bowl. She indicated the glop, her words apprehensive. "This is that temporary color, right?"

Gia nodded. "Demi-permanent. It'll wash out in about four weeks. Sooner if you really hate it. Stop worrying."

"I'll try." She squinted at it again, then sat back, horrified. "Is *that* the color my hair will be?"

"No, Em," Gia said with exaggerated patience. "I wouldn't dye your hair deathbed gray. Give me a little credit, at least."

"Sorry." Emie held out her hands and took a deep breath. "Okay. I'm okay."

"Again, not that my opinion counts for much, but I think you look sexy as hell in your glasses," Gia said lightly, setting the bowl on the table and digging neat squares of aluminum foil out of the tackle box. She placed them next to the bowl, then stepped behind Emie and parted her hair neatly with a yellow comb, clamping one side of it in some kind of big clothespin-looking thing.

Her opinion meant a lot, more than any other woman's ever had, but Emie couldn't bring herself to admit that. Instead she quipped, "Well, you know what they say. Women don't make passes at girls who wear glasses."

"I think the quote was actually *men* don't make passes, but whatever. And maybe women like Elizalde, *que malcreado*, may not, but that's her loss." She lifted a section of Emie's hair, wove the skinny end of a rat-tail comb through the strands, then slathered dye on it from the roots out. She folded the section in one of the foil squares and neatly folded the ends.

"And women like you, Gia?" Emie ventured, her pulse drumming at her throat. "Somehow I just can't imagine you'd go for the bookish, couldn't-care-less type when all the best-looking women are throwing themselves at you."

"Women *like me*?" She laughed. "What do you mean by that?"

What could Emie say? Drop-dead gorgeous women? Those who should never be more than half dressed? Toned, tawny goddesses hot enough to have cold water dumped over their white T-shirts in a soft drink commercial? Make-me-shiver-and-beg type of women? "You know." She sniffed, the pungent chemicals stinging her nose. "You're not exactly…average."

Gia deftly separated, painted, and foiled more of Emie's hair, her fingers sure and gentle. "If that is your version of a compliment, *Profé*, thank you. And incidentally, just because a woman wears glasses doesn't mean she's a bookish, couldn't-care-less type."

Emie didn't want to argue the virtues—or not—of her spectacles anymore. "Tell me about your family." She couldn't see Gia's face, but noticed that Gia seemed to ponder her request before answering, taking her time to color and wrap another section of her hair.

"There's not much to tell. What do you want to know?"

"You know, the usual. Where were you born, where are your parents, do you have any brothers and sisters."

"I never knew my father," she started, dipping the little brush into the plastic bowl. "My brother Phillipe and I grew up with my mom in Chicago."

"Does she still live there?"

"She passed away four years ago."

Silence.

Hair dye.

Foil.

"I'm so sorry," Emie whispered, awkward to her core. "How rude of me to pry."

"*No te preocupes*. You weren't prying. We're getting to know each other. It's what people do. Anyhow, I'm sorry, too. She had a hard life, so I don't blame her for checking out early." Gia paused, resting the heels of her hands against Emie's scalp. "But, God, I miss her."

"I bet she misses you and Phillipe, too."

Gia scoffed and resumed working on her hair. "My brother and I didn't make life any easier for her, that's for damn sure. Until we grew up, of course. Phillipe was always a pretty good son. Me, on the other hand—" She sucked in one side of her cheek, making a sound of regret.

"Were you a bad girl, Gia?" Emie teased.

A tense pause stretched between them.

"Actually…I was. Not my proudest memory."

Gia's somber tone straightened Emie up and warned her to move away from the subject. "And Phillipe? Where is he?"

"He's a missionary with the church. Lives in Venezuela."

"*¿A lucerio?*"

"Yes, really." Gia chuckled. "Is that such a surprise?"

"You just don't seem...priestly to me. Or nunly, not that nunly's a real word." *What a waste that would be*, she thought, waiting for lightning to strike.

"*Phillipe's* the missionary, Emie, not me."

She leaned her head back. "Yes, but. Well. I guess you're right. Does he look like a male version of you?"

"Kind of." She dipped out more dye. "Shorter hair, obviously. Why?"

She faced forward again and hiked one shoulder up. "I don't know. Seems unfair for the Venezuelan women. A male missionary who looked anything like you would make them want to sin, not repent."

Gia laughed again, and Emie's cheeks heated. Where were these bold comments coming from? One would almost think she was flirting with the woman. Curiosity getting the better of her, she said, "Tell me about this bad-girl past of yours. I'm intrigued."

"Oh, sure, *scandalosa*. Dig out all my skeletons."

Emie clicked her tongue. "I am not a gossip! I'm just making friendly conversation. It's what people do."

"Uh-huh." Gia had finished applying the color and foil to her hair, and reached for a timer. Its gentle ticking and the whir of the refrigerator filled the air. "If I tell you about my past, you've got to answer any question I ask you. Okay? Just one."

"*Any* question? How can that be fair?"

"Take it or leave it," Gia said playfully, leaning her hip against the counter and crossing her arms.

Emie's lips parted. Before she could answer, a knock on the back screen door interrupted them.

"Em?" Paloma sounded teary.

Both Gia and Emie turned. "Paloma," Emie said, reaching from under the cape to put on her glasses. "What's wrong? Come in." She stood and crossed to the door.

Paloma's puffy cheeks and red-rimmed eyes showed she'd

been crying. Pep shuffled in next to her, his head bowed. Paloma's protective hand cupped his tiny neck. "I'm sorry to interrupt. Hi, Gia," she added, distractedly.

"Hey."

"You're not interrupting, honey, you know that," Emie added, turning her attention to the boy. She softened her tone and squatted to his level. "Hey, Pep. Aren't you going to say hi to your auntie?"

His head came up slowly, and he did a double-take at her foil-wrapped hair and black plastic cape. His pout brightened tentatively. "Cool. You look like a creepy space man."

"Coming from you, *m'ijo*, that's great praise." Emie noted the deep purple bruising around Pep's eye, the fresh cuts over his brow and on his swollen lip. She flickered a glance at Gia, who was studying the boy's face with a concerned frown. "And you look like a heavyweight boxer, kiddo. What happened?"

"I don't wanna talk 'bout it." Pep's scowl deepened.

"It's okay, baby," Paloma said, her voice wobbly from holding back tears. "You go in the living room and watch TV while I talk to Auntie Emie and Gia. Later I'll take you to McDonald's, okay?"

Pep shrugged, then scuffed listlessly out of the room.

"Where's Teddy?"

"I dropped him off at my mom's." She stared wistfully at the doorway through which her older son had left. "I figured Pep could use some one-on-one time."

"Can I pour you a cup of coffee, Paloma?" Gia asked.

She nodded before slumping into a chair at the end of the table and dissolving into tears, her face in her palms. Paloma's shoulders shook as she wept.

Emie scraped a chair over until it faced Paloma, then laid her hands on her friend's knee. "Honey, what happened? The same boys again?"

She nodded. "He's just a baby, for God's sake. Why is this happening?"

Gia set the mug in front of Paloma, then laid her hand on Emie's shoulder, intending to let her know she'd wait in the other room. Gia's insides knotted whenever she saw a woman cry. She should give the two friends privacy.

Emie peered up at her, expression disturbed. Before Gia could take her leave, Emie covered her hand with her own and said, "Pep's been having trouble with some bullies in their neighborhood. He's been coming home beat up all summer long. This is his fourth—"

"Fifth," Paloma corrected.

"His fifth black eye since school let out."

"And he's six. *Six!* His permanent teeth are just starting to come in, and I'm afraid he's gonna get them knocked out." Paloma sniffed loudly, then smeared at her eyes. "He's such a peaceful, introverted little guy. What's with young kids, Gia? Do you know? Why do they always pick on the weaker ones?"

A feeling like a steel-toed boot kicked Gia's gut. She sank into a chair and smoothed a palm down her face. If they only knew they were talking to the grown-up version of one of Pep's tormenters. A tidal wave of guilt engulfed her. She felt like a fraud. "I don't know, Paloma. Have you or your wife talked it over with Pep yet?" *Way to go, G, pawn it off.*

Paloma's eyes flashed. "That's another thing." She glowered at Emie, flailing her small hands to punctuate her emphatic words. "She has time to solve all the problems in the world, but she can't take half a day to stay home and talk to her son."

Emie glanced at Gia again, twisting her mouth to the side. "Deanne is a cop with the Denver force. We all went to high school together," she explained, her eyes conveying more than her words did. "Her...schedule keeps her away from home a lot."

Chipper cartoon voices and zany sound effects filtered in from the living room, oddly out of sync with the gravity of the conversation. If Paloma and Deanne had argued that morning, Gia felt certain she—being an outsider—stood way on the wrong side of enemy lines. Emie and Paloma watched as she geared up to traipse through a verbal mine field in this partner war. Woefully unarmed, Gia swallowed and took one tentative step, bracing herself mentally for the explosion.

"Maybe she's really busy at work. A lot of police departments are understaffed these days. I'm sure she'd stay home if she could," Gia offered, not sure at all. She didn't even know Deanne. The woman could be a complete asshole, for all she knew. All Gia could give Paloma were air balloons of false assurances, weightless and empty and trite.

No mines blew, though, thank God. Paloma half laughed, half huffed at Gia's suggestion. "Yeah, it's just swell for the boys having a 'tough butch' for a mom when she can't even help them escape the neighborhood jerks." She reached for a piece of cake and nibbled at it halfheartedly.

Gia tiptoed over one mine and faced another. She had no business offering anyone parenting or marital advice. But Emie— wide-eyed and serious despite the glob of purplish gray dye meandering down her temple from her berserk silver crown— kept looking at her like she should save the day. And, damnit, she didn't want to let Emie down.

She stood, pointing vaguely at the doorway. "Why don't you two talk for a while? I'll go hang out with Pep." Gia jerked her head toward the ticking timer. "Call me when that goes off so I can rinse you."

"I will," Emie said distractedly.

"Don't forget unless you want to fry your hair."

"I won't. I promise. Go talk to Pep." She smiled like Gia was a knight riding her shining steed in to rescue the little prince. Tenderness welled inside Gia to the exploding point. She leaned toward Emie, wanting so badly to capture those red apple lips with her own. Instead, she flicked the blob of dye off her temple.

"She's so kind," Gia heard Paloma murmur as she left the room.

Gia's heart pounded an army cadence as she marched

toward the front of the house. She paused in the hallway. What in the hell should she say? Long pause. *What would you have wanted to hear as a confused six-year-old, G?* She didn't think she would've wanted to hear much of anything from an adult, unfortunately. As a child, she'd yearned simply to be *listened to* more than anything else. She'd just wanted someone to hear her. With that in mind, she forged ahead. How scary could a six-year-old pipsqueak be, after all?

Gia stopped in the archway to the living room and leaned one shoulder against the wall, crossing her arms. Pep slumped on the sofa enveloped in his stylish baggy clothes. The animated action on the screen prompted no emotion on his innocent, battered face. Bright colors shone in his listless round eyes. His bottom lip jutted out and his shoulders hung. He looked depressed. At six years of age, that was just goddamned unacceptable. Pep stole a sidelong peek at Gia, trying to pretend he hadn't.

"Órale, chavalito." Gia pushed off the wall and sauntered toward the young boy.

He blinked, solemn. "They kick you out?"

"Something like that."

Pep pursed his lips. *"Chismas* time. No one allowed except Auntie Emie or Auntie Iris," the boy added, his tone resigned and knowledgeable.

Gossip time. Gia grinned at Pep's assessment of his mother's discussions with her friends. She settled onto the couch next to the tiny boy, mimicking his position. Pep's feet didn't come close to reaching the floor, a detail Gia found overwhelmingly endearing. He looked too small to be targeted by bullies. Her fists clenched of their own volition. She fought to relax them.

For a few minutes, they just stared at the screen together. Gia gave the boy time to wonder what the heck this weird grown-up was doing next to him. "What're we watching?" she finally asked.

Pep's feet bounced three times, then stopped. His eyes remained on the screen. "Somethin', I dunno."

Gia scooped up the remote. "If it's that boring, then maybe we should watch a soap opera."

"No, please no!" Pep whined, reaching for the remote. He wore the desperate look of a boy who'd suffered through one too many of the sappy shows.

"Aw, come on, how about one with girls crying and lots of kissing?" Gia mimicked a few big loud smackeroos in the air.

A grudging smile lifted one corner of Pep's mouth, tugging at an angry-looking cut that had puffed his bottom lip. "No way. I don't like those shows. Let's watch this."

Gia shrugged and handed the boy the remote. "Your choice, big guy." She stretched her arms up, then interlaced her fingers behind her head.

Pep hugged the remote to his bony chest. Pretty soon he set it down, then stretched his arms up and interlaced his fingers behind his own head. He peeked over at Gia. "Aren't you that one with the black Ford truck?"

"That's me."

"I forget, was it an extra cab or a crew cab?"

"Extra cab."

Pep pondered this. "You know the crew cab has real back seats 'steada jump seats," he said, tone matter-of-fact. "If you got kids, you should get the crew cab. Got kids?"

"Nope." She angled a glance at the boy. "You?"

Pep giggled at the absurdity. "What's your name again?"

"Gia."

"Gia," Pep repeated, as though trying out the sound on his tongue. "Am I allowed to call you that?"

Gia lowered her arms, then lifted one ankle to rest across the opposite knee. "Sure."

"You got that Ford truck here right now, Gia?"

"Mm-hmm."

His interest piqued, Pep stretched his neck up to peer out the front window, then whipped back toward Gia. "I don't see it parked out there."

"It's in the back," Gia told him. "I live here."

The boy's eyes widened and his jaw dropped. "You live with my auntie Emie? Are you her wife?"

Gia barked a laugh. "Slow down, buddy. I haven't even kissed her yet."

"Yuck." He blinked up at Gia with pure innocence and thinly veiled disgust. "That's sick. What does kissing have to do with bein' a wife?"

Gia narrowed her eyes with playful menace. "You want me to turn on that soap opera, buddy?"

Pep's missing teeth gave his grin the look of a seven-ten split. "Naw."

"Then quit flappin' and watch your show."

Pep giggled again. A few cartoon-filled quiet moments passed before he lost his ability to sit without speaking. "Are you Auntie Emie's *auntie*?" he asked.

"Nope." Gia frowned. "Sheesh, how old do I look?"

"I dunno." Pep shrugged. "Just regular old. As old as any other grown-up." He touched his swollen lip gently, then checked his fingers for blood. "You her cousin?"

"Nope."

He cocked his head to the side. "Her sister?"

Gia glanced at him with lighthearted exasperation. "I'll make you a deal, Pep, how's that? I'll answer your questions if you answer a few of mine." She offered her palm.

"Deal." The handshake engulfed the little boy's hand. "So, are you?"

"Am I what?"

Pep rolled his eyes. "Auntie Emie's sister."

Gia sighed and ruffled the boy's hair. "Sometimes it feels like it, *chavalito*, but no, I'm not her sister."

❖

Emie offered a listening ear and a shoulder to cry on until Paloma felt a little better, infinitely stronger. With a long exhale, her tiny friend raised her gaze to her foiled locks. "So, wow. Science fiction. What's this gonna look like, Em?"

She stood and carried their dishes to the sink, then turned back. "Who knows, but the official color is eggplant."

"Ay." Paloma cringed. "What did Iris say?"

It was a given that she'd consulted their resident supermodel. They generally expected her to know everything about everything having to do with grooming. And she generally did. "She said it will look good, it's a popular color or some such nonsense." The timer read ten minutes. "Anyway, anything new should work to kick Vitoria in the ass for what she did to me."

Paloma tilted her head to the side. "Aw, honey, don't say that. When are you gonna open your eyes? Forget Elizalde. It's so freaking obvious Gia's into you. Having a red-hot woman like her on your arm is the best revenge."

Emie closed her eyes and mentally counted. "Paloma, I don't want to get into this with both you and Iris in the same morning, okay? I have to do what I have to do. Period."

"You still think Gia is here out of some sense of guilt?"

"Yes." *Pause.* "No." *Sigh.* "Hell, I don't know." She dropped back into the chair. "She's nice to me. We're friends."

"So, why don't you—"

"Friends, Paloma, that's all," she affirmed. "She's not my girlfriend, I don't *want* a girlfriend, and I have to even the score with Vitoria the way I see fit."

"Even the score." Paloma scoffed, but held her hands up in surrender, turning her face to the side. "Look, forget I said anything. I love you, Emie."

"I know. I love you, too."

"You're a genius, you're funny, you're kind." She ticked Emie's assets off with her fingers. "You have a great career, a gorgeous house."

"That's not the—"

"And *I*," Paloma continued, "know how amazing you are."

Emie smiled a little sadly. "Well, if I could see myself through your eyes, maybe I wouldn't be trussed up like a futuristic turkey. But I can't, so I am. End of story." Her voice dropped to a whisper. "Please just support me."

"You know I do." Paloma snagged another piece of coffee cake off the platter. "I just worry for you."

"Well, don't." Emie checked the timer again. Five minutes to go. "I'm going to get Gia now. I don't like the idea of having all my hair fall out. Be right back."

Emie could hear the ebb and flow of conversation as she approached, and she slowed her steps so as not to interrupt. She hung back, just outside the living room, peeking around the corner. Gia and Pep sat side by side in the exact same position— one ankle across the opposite knee.

Pep, looking endearingly tiny next to Gia's sculpted bod, stared with rapt attention at his new friend. "So, if you aren't Auntie Emie's sister or auntie or wife, what are you?"

"I'm her friend," Gia said easily.

The boy screwed up his face and pulled his head back. "Huh? You live with her!"

Emie ducked back and covered her mouth to muffle a laugh.

"So? You can live with friends, Pep."

"But who'd want to? First you hafta be friends with 'em, then you hafta buy 'em stuff. Sooner or later you gotta kiss 'em."

Gia chuckled. "Once you get older you'll realize that doesn't happen nearly as often as you'd like, my pal."

"Sick. I don't want it to happen ever."

"Yeah? Talk to me in ten years about that," Gia murmured, her tone wry. Her voice changed when she added, "Okay, my turn for a question." A beat passed. "What's up with the bruises, guy? Who's giving you a hard time?"

"I don't wanna talk about it," Pep groused.

Gia's voice rumbled smoothly through the room. "We had a deal, Pep. Remember? I answered your questions, now you answer mine."

Pep clicked his tongue, sounding dejected. Even at six, he couldn't bring himself to welch on a deal. "I don't do nothin' to those kids, Gia," he said in a plaintive tone. "They just don't like me. They don't like that I have a mom and a mama. They call me a freak and a queer, and they won't leave me alone."

"You know them from school?"

"Nuh-uh, they're way older. Like, nine." Awe laced his words. "They started calling me mama's boy and sissy, and now they say I'm a snitch because my other mommy's a police officer. They call me bad words I'm not allowed to say. And they call Mommy and Mama bad words, too."

Emie could feel Gia's underlying outrage from where she stood. She didn't even have to see her face. Her ability to hide it from Pep was impressive, though. "And you walk away?" Gia asked, her voice level.

"I try," Pep said, "but they grab me."

Emie peered around the corner again. Gia had turned toward Pep and rested one arm along the back of the sofa. She looked intently at the boy.

"Have you talked to your mama about this? Or your mom?"

"A little, when she's home. Mom tells me to stand up to them…but I'm afraid," he finished, his voice a shame-riddled whisper. Emie could see the boy's swollen lip quiver from her hiding place, and a bolt of anger at Deanne shot through her. How could the woman tell an innocent little child like Pep to "stand up"? She never thought she'd utter these words about another woman, but…macho jackass.

Gia nudged Pep's chin up with her knuckle until the boy met her gaze. "It's okay to be afraid, *chavalito*. You hold on to that fear."

"But Mom's not afraid of nothing. She's a police officer."

Gia shook her head. "Everyone's afraid of something, Pep. It doesn't make you less of a man to admit it."

"Well, I'm afraid to stand up to 'em, then," Pep muttered. "I don't know how to fight."

"What your mom is trying to tell you is not to fight back with fists, you fight back with this." Gia pointed at her temple.

"My head?"

"Your brain. Your smarts."

Pep fidgeted. "Whaddya mean?"

"A lot of bullies act mean because they don't have a lot of smarts, they're empty up there."

Pep's eyes widened with horror. "They don't got insides? Like brains?"

Gia chuckled. "No, I meant they don't have anything in their hearts. No love, no feelings. You understand?"

Pep nodded.

"They try to make themselves feel better by pushing around smaller people. Better people." Gia lowered her chin and her tone. "But you, you're a smart guy, yeah?"

Pep beamed. "Yeah."

"Don't ever let them make you doubt what's inside here." She tapped the little boy's chest. "You have love and feelings in your heart, Pep. A family that loves you. Don't let those kids put their anger inside you. You might have to keep walking away for now. But, eventually, if you do that, they'll leave you alone. Once they do, forget about them. When they pick on you, it's their problem, not yours."

"For reals?" He slanted a glance at Gia. "You for sure think my mom won't mind if I don't fight 'em?"

"I think your mom and mama will both be proud if you're brave enough to use your wits instead of your fists." She smiled. "I know I would be."

"What's wits?"

Gia pointed at her temple again.

Pep brightened. "Same as smarts?"

"You got it." Gia laid her palm on the boy's head.

Emie froze to the spot, her chest tight. Was there anything this gentle, sweet, intelligent woman couldn't do? Emie wanted to hug her. She wanted to shower kisses on her beautiful face. She wanted to climb on her lap and—

Ding! The timer brought Gia's gaze to the doorway.

Shit. Caught.

Emie stepped into the arch and bestowed a wan smile, forcing back the waves of desire and awe before Gia noticed. She cleared her throat. "The, ah, eggplant appears to be done."

CHAPTER SIX

The first things Gia had noticed about Emie were her clear intelligence, genuineness, and wit. She respected Emie more than any woman she'd ever met, and she was drawn to her personality, without a doubt. But, the more Gia was around Emie, the more the physical attraction blossomed, and she'd begun to fixate on a deep desire to touch her. Emie had no idea how sexy she was. Gia made no apologies for wanting her, but the forced platonic stipulation in their relationship posed a bit of an obstacle to acting on those yearnings.

Pep and Paloma had left, and Gia was doing her best not to stare at Emie's shapely ass as she bent over the sink rinsing her hair. She wore low-slung denim better than any woman Gia had ever seen. Not tight, but clinging just enough to provide a mystery to ponder as she fell asleep at night. Baggy enough to maintain the signature demureness that had begun to drive Gia to distraction with wanting her.

She *wanted* Emie.

God, she wanted her.

The black plastic cape had fallen open, allowing a glimpse of Emie's trim waist. Tiny, almost invisible hairs dusted her lower back. Dumbstruck, Gia ached to feel them. To slip her hand around Emie's soft, flat tummy and pull the alluring professor against her own body. Move against her until she understood just how much Gia desired her, how intensely Emie turned her on.

"So, how does it look?"

Gia jerked her lust-filled gaze away. "W-what?"

Emie flipped her head up, wound it in a towel, swami-style, and turned. A delicate blush colored her cheeks. "The eggplant," she replied, as though it should have been obvious. "Do I look ridiculous? Tell the truth."

Gia swallowed past her tight, dry throat, thirsting for something that wasn't hers to take. From what she'd seen of the hair color, it looked rich and shiny. Emie would love it. But Gia was too distracted to care at the moment.

"We have to style it first. But I promise you don't look ridiculous. Why don't you go get your blow-dryer?" she suggested, turning away to gather her supplies. She took her time, willing the unabashed look of lust from her expression so she could think clearly.

Gia didn't know how much more of this pretending to be *just* Emie's friend she could handle. She wanted her, damnit. Was that so wrong? Should fate deny her the possibility of a deeper relationship with this amazing woman simply because of their unfortunate beginning? Gia wanted to court and seduce her, to see those bright gentle eyes looking deeply into her own as they made love, connected in that all-consuming way nothing else could replace.

The bitch of it was, Emie didn't even intend to entice her. But the guilelessness only served to intensify Gia's feelings. She liked everything about Emie, from her seriousness to her wit. Her neat-as-a-pin house, the strength of her friendships, and the obvious solidity of her upbringing. She was unlike anyone Gia had ever met. She wanted to be Emie's friend, sure, but she wanted more, too. So much more.

She'd come to Colorado on impulse seeking a woman who'd intrigued her. But she'd found a woman she knew, in time, she could love. With her whole soul.

Damn, that was scary.

She didn't even know if she could live up to being the kind of woman Emie deserved.

Okay, deep breath.

She was getting way ahead of herself. Distance. That's what she needed. Space to gather her—

Emie's arm snaked around her waist, and every rational thought within Gia ground to a shuddering, mind-bending halt. Emie's warm, pliant, lavender-scented body molded against her back, and she felt Emie's cheek press against her shoulder blade. She grew vaguely aware of the wet hair towel dampening her shirt, but didn't care. She sank into the embrace, closed her eyes.

Was this real or a cruelly vivid mental manifestation of her wishes?

"You have no idea how touched I am by what you did for Pep," Emie whispered, her breath a warm tickle on Gia's back.

Gia didn't speak, didn't move, didn't want to break the spell of this precious moment.

"I didn't mean to eavesdrop, Gia, but I'm so glad I did. I…I have never known a person as kind as you, as selfless as you were to that battered little boy."

I'm no better than the boys who beat him up.

The insidious thought needled Gia. She pushed it away. "I didn't do anything special, *querida*. Please don't give me credit I don't deserve." She reached her arm back and pressed Emie more tightly against her, tilting her head back.

"How can you say that?" Emie murmured. "He wouldn't open up to his mama or Deanne. He wouldn't talk to me. But I walk into that room and you have him eating out of your hand."

"My truck." Gia cleared her throat. "He just likes the truck. It was a bonding thing."

Emie sighed. "Whatever it was, I'm impressed. And appreciative. And so…I don't have words. Just…thank you. So much. You'd make a great mother someday, Gia."

A raw sensual image of Emie heavy with their child weakened Gia's knees. She couldn't formulate the words to respond.

"And, despite how we met, I'm so glad we're friends," Emie added firmly, releasing Gia from the unexpected embrace.

Friends.

The word hung in the air like a brick room divider, the moment lost. Before she recovered from mourning the loss of contact, Emie had slipped away and out of the room. Gia whirled around, thinking perhaps she'd imagined it all. But, no. The air cooled the wet spot the towel had left on her shirt. She reached over her shoulder and touched the damp fabric absentmindedly.

Emie had hugged her. Breathed against her skin.

She'd connected. Now she was gone.

Gia bent forward and leaned her elbows on the counter, hanging her head. Her dye-stained hands wound into involuntary fists, she clenched her teeth. What a fool. She'd read more into a spontaneous moment than she should've, and now she felt like she'd been tied to the tracks and run over by a high-speed emotional roller coaster. Repeatedly.

"Fuck," she rasped through her teeth.

Emie wanted to be *friends*.

And Gia wanted to please Emie.

Stalemate.

So, okay, she'd back off and be her goddamned friend. Fine. But she'd need some emotional and physical distance in order to pull it off. Bottom line, she couldn't be around Emie any longer and not want more than just friendship. She was that far gone.

And she needed a shower. Cold.

Not to mention a vibrator. Turbo.

Half an hour later, her hair dried and styled, Emie stood in front of the bathroom mirror. "I love it. I really do." She turned her face side to side and admired the subtle berry shimmer on her cropped locks. "Eggplant. Who would've thought…?"

"I'm glad you approve."

"You know why I like it?" she continued, trying not to be concerned by the fact that Gia seemed so distant and eager to get away from her. Did she resent having been pushed into the position of dealing with Pep? Maybe she didn't like children. Maybe she didn't want that much inclusion in Emie's personal life. "I like it b-because it looks like me, but…better," she said, trying to hint about the rest of the makeover. She hoped Gia would tone down the original version of exotic a bit.

"Yes, it does," Gia said, not really looking at her. "Look like you, I mean. But don't sweat it, we'll go a little bolder with the style for the fall faculty get-together, maybe with some spikes."

Emie's hands froze in mid-primp. "Spikes?"

Gia nodded, a muscle in her jaw working as she swept Emie with an objective, assessing look. "Maybe shimmer spray, too. We want you to stand out so Elizalde can't help but notice you."

So much for the idea of toning down. Clearly, Gia found these subtle changes in her appearance too boring compared to the va-va-voom women from El Chapultepec she'd liked so much.

Emie stifled a sigh. Ridiculous or not, it irked her to think about Gia lusting over those overblown seductresses. Gia might think they looked exotic, but Emie thought they looked phony. Desperate. She could never look anywhere near as…ripe. She didn't even want to. How had she gone from being a career-focused, confident woman into someone so fixated on her damned appearance? Ludicrous.

None of this fluff should matter. She'd already told Gia she didn't want her, and judging from the woman's current distant attitude, Gia had obviously realized Emie wasn't her type either. Well, what had she really expected?

Enough, Em. She had revenge to seek.

Gia's feelings about her were inconsequential in the scheme of things. Besides, if she just accepted the woman's judgment about the makeover, no matter the results, maybe Gia would start to see her in a different light, unobstructed by guilt or pity or whatever it was that had prompted her to quit her job and drive to Colorado, of all things. And, with any luck, she'd stop looking as if she'd rather be anywhere but here.

Emie turned, resting her butt lightly on the vanity. "You know what? You're right. I'd love spikes."

Gia's brows rose, almost startled. "Yeah?"

"The bolder the better."

Suspicion claimed Gia's expression. "Since when?"

"Since, I don't know"—she shrugged—"now. What have I got to lose? Bring on the spikes." She grinned. "Show me the leather."

The room fell silent, but for the drip in the old sink that she'd kept meaning to fix. She'd expected a more effusive approval reaction. Instead Gia stared at her, face completely devoid of expression.

Emie spread her arms. "What? I thought you'd be glad I decided to go for it. Isn't that the point? Don't you want me to look exotic?"

After another moment, Gia cleared her throat and touched Emie's arm. "No, I do. I want you to be happy and look…exactly how you want to look. You just surprised me, that's all." A wry smile lifted one corner of her mouth. "You seem to have a knack for that."

❖

The afternoon sun beat down as Emie marched toward the carriage house with a mission and a goal: to find out why Gia had been avoiding her and to make her stop. Damnit, she missed Gia's company. She hadn't seen her for more than a couple of minutes at a time in the past several days, and Gia had yet to comment on her contact lenses.

Why?

What had she done?

It seemed ever since Gia'd gotten roped into the middle of Pep's problems, she'd made herself conspicuously scarce. Instead of hanging out with Emie, Gia split her time between holing up in the carriage house and repairing things around *her* house. While Emie appreciated all Gia had done, she'd gladly keep her squeaky door, dripping faucets, and loose porch slats just to get inside Gia's head a little bit, figure her out.

Knock, knock, knock.

She stepped back from the arch-top front door of the carriage house and tried to slow her breathing. Shuffling accompanied by muffled Zydeco music sounded beyond the entrance. Footsteps approached, the deadbolt jangled, then—

Pause. Awkwardness.

"Hey," Gia said, blinking, distracted. Clearly she was surprised by Emie's unexpected appearance on her stoop.

An overpowering odor of paints and turpentine wafted out, burning Emie's eyes. She stepped back and inhaled fresh air.

"Are you okay?" Gia whipped a glance over her shoulder, then squeezed out the door and closed it behind her. "Sorry about the smell. I just get used to it, but I know it can be pretty bad." Barefooted, Gia wore those torn Levi's jeans she loved so much, an equally tattered tank top, and not much else unless paint smears counted as accessories.

"It's okay. I'm fine. I just...haven't seen much of you." *Pathetic.* Emie's shoulders raised and dropped. "We're neighbors now, so I thought I'd come over and say hi." Okay, this was uncomfortable as hell. Was Gia going to invite her in? Didn't seem like it. Emie crossed her arms. "So...hi."

Gia's eyes warmed and a slow smile spanned her face. "Hi."

"Are you busy?" Emie's gaze darted to the closed door behind her, then back to her face.

"I'm, uh"—Gia rubbed her jawline with the back of her hand, then jabbed a thumb over her shoulder—"working."

"I figured as much. How's that going?"

"Great." Her expression sparkled. "I have a couple of gallery owners interested in looking at a few of my pieces. I might get a few showings, maybe some sales."

"That's wonderful!" Emie exclaimed, clapping her hands together. Suddenly she didn't feel so ignored. If Gia established herself in the arts community, that just might give her incentive to stay after the makeover agreement ended. Hell, she'd keep her around however she could. "When will you know more?"

"I'm not sure. I've been working like a madwoman to get everything ready." Her gaze darted to the ground. "I guess that's why I've been…uh, not around."

"It's okay," Emie said, not quite believing the excuse. "You don't owe me an explanation, and what better reason?" *I just miss you so desperately*, she wanted to add. But didn't. "I'm proud of you."

Gia searched her face, then reached out and ran the pads of her fingers down Emie's cheek. The touch was unexpected and brief. Devastating and sexy, too. "Are we still on for makeup shopping tomorrow?"

Emie's face tingled and her mouth had gone dry. "Of course, if you have time, that is."

"I wouldn't want to spend the day any other way."

Really? Yeah, officially confused. Gia didn't seem to be angry with her; in fact, she seemed almost happy Emie had come by. So why had Gia stopped meeting her on the back porch for coffee each morning? It couldn't just be the artwork. Everyone had to take a break now and then. "Okay. Good." She hesitated, wanting to say more but feeling unsure. If she'd done anything to insult Gia—

"Something on your mind?"

"No." Emie paused. "Well, actually, yes." She laughed a little. "I just thought you might like to come up to the house for dinner."

For a split second, Gia looked stricken, then it passed. "Oh, you know, I've got so much work..."

"Come on, Gia. Paloma and the kids are coming over. Iris was going to join us but she had to cancel." She assessed Gia's reaction to this, but she didn't seem put off by the idea of a group get-together. In fact, her regal features fell into something suspiciously reminiscent of relief. "I know Pep will be disappointed if you aren't there. You're his new superhero, you know."

Gia scoffed. "Trust me, I'm no superhero."

Emie lifted her chin, ready for disappointment, but her words barreled forth. "We could rent a movie afterward. It's probably not a night on the town like you're used to, but—"

Gia laid her fingers across Emie's lips to stop her words, then said, "Stop convincing me. I'd love to come."

"You would? Really?"

"Really."

"Great." She fought to tamp down her enthusiasm. No sense looking like she was used to rejection. "Okay, then." She started to walk away, then turned back. "Seven o'clock?"

Gia reached up and braced her arm at the top of the doorjamb, molten gaze boring into her. "How about six?"

"Six? Oh. Well. I won't have everything ready by then. Everyone else is coming at seven." She moved to nudge her glasses up. They weren't there. Instead, she wound her hands into a clasp behind her back and pasted a wan smile on her face. "Can't get used to the no-glasses thing."

"Understandable. But six is even better. I'll help you cook."

"Cook?" Emie balked. "Are you sure?"

"Em..." Gia said, the word sounding more like a sigh.

Emie wasn't quite sure what Gia meant by breathing her name out like that. She only knew she needed to get away and do a little breathing herself. The woman really disconcerted her. "Okay, you win. Six o'clock."

"Great. Can I bring anything?"

"Just…you, G. Just you." *That's all I need.* She started back up the path toward her house, feeling giddy-to-bursting, like she'd won a prize and was fighting not to gloat. Her body wanted to break into a run but she wound tight fists at her sides and concentrated on measuring her steps.

"Querida." The word, Gia's caressing voice, stopped Emie cold. Her heart began to hammer. "I've always been fond of your glasses, you know that. But the contacts look great, too."

Emie turned slowly and their gazes met and held. If she didn't know better, she could swear Gia looked as if she wanted to close the distance between them and kiss her. But how could that be when she'd been avoiding her like a communicable disease for the past several days? Emie's panic revved, urging her to flee before she threw herself at Gia. The compliment wrapped around her like a hug. "Thank you," she said finally, reaching up to tuck a lock of hair that didn't need to be tucked behind her ear. "I like them."

❖

Gia rubbed her palms together and glanced around the kitchen. "All right, Sous Chef Mendez at your service and ready to cook. What can I do?"

Golden light softened the edges of the room and Norah Jones's mellifluous voice permeated the air. Emie wore a long, fluttery wine-colored skirt covered in little blue flowers and a matching blue T-shirt. A flour sack apron covered most of the outfit, and the "hominess" of it cheered Gia. Emie's sandals exposed shiny clear-polished toenails, and the whole room smelled like her signature lavender scent. The situation—and the company—was so conducive to romance, Gia thanked God that Paloma and the boys would arrive soon to act as a buffer.

"Hmm, well, you can pour us each a glass of wine, and then it's your choice." She gestured with a chef's knife. "Season the steaks, chop the carrots, toss the salad, or fix the potatoes. Dessert is already finished."

"I make a killer glazed carrot," Gia said, opening one cupboard, then another until she happened upon the wine goblets. She slipped two stems between her fingers and lowered them on the countertop. "How about I make those and the steaks, you take care of the salad and potatoes?"

"Deal."

They worked in companionable silence for several minutes until most of the prep work was done. Emie picked up her wineglass and sat gratefully in a chair, rotating her ankles. "Nothing else to do until they arrive," she said. "I don't want to overcook the meat."

Gia took the chair across from her. "It feels good to relax, yeah?" She glanced around, shoulders raising, then dropping with a sigh. "I like your house."

"What a nice thing to say." Emie smiled. "I like it, too. Especially since you've fixed all the little irritations lately. You know, you didn't have to do that."

Gia shrugged off her compliment. *"De nada."*

Emie glanced at the clock, hoping Paloma had gotten the kids bustled into the car without much trouble. "I have to warn you, Paloma's boys are picky eaters. And that may be an understatement." She twisted her mouth to the side. "I never know from one day to the next what they'll like."

"Eh, kids. I was one once." She sipped from her wineglass, studying her over the rim. "How's Pep, by the way?"

"Well, I know you don't like praise, but Paloma says he's more upbeat than he's been in a long time"—a pause ensued—"ever since you talked to him."

"I'm glad," Gia said, but a shadow crossed over her expression and she changed the subject quickly. "Tell me about Paloma's wife. Deanne, isn't it?"

"Yeah." Emie flipped her hand and leaned the back of her head against the wall. "Not much to say, really. Deanne and Paloma have been together since we were all in eighth grade, if I remember correctly. The only lesbian couple in our school who were out and didn't care about the talk." She bracketed those words with air quotes. "They were the perfect couple, you know? And eventually almost everybody accepted them. We always knew they'd be together forever." She crossed her legs, rustling her skirt.

"But…?" Gia urged.

Emie sipped, wondering how Gia had known she had more to say. "It's just my opinion, and I would never say anything to Paloma, but Deanne doesn't pay attention to her like she used to. I know she has a busy, demanding job—"

"She works the street?"

Emie nodded, eyes focused on her wineglass. She twirled the stem in her fingers thoughtfully. "She probably always will. Likes the adrenaline rush, I guess. Anyway, if you ask me, Dee takes Paloma and the kids for granted."

"That's a shame."

"They'll work it out." She set her glass aside and met Gia's gaze squarely. "They always do."

Gia reached across the table and covered Emie's hand with her own. "What about you, *querida*? Why haven't you settled down with the perfect woman?"

A deep flush rose to Emie's face. Where the heck had that come from? "I guess I haven't found the perfect woman."

A smile invited her dimple. "The standard answer."

"Okay, the truth?" Emie sniffed and withdrew her hand, a little self-conscious but not wanting to hide herself. This was her—a wallflower. An outsider. Single by choice. If Gia was truly her friend, it wouldn't matter. She twisted her mouth to the side. "I've never been in a serious relationship."

"Never?"

Emie shook her head. "In high school…no one asked me out.

Then there was college and graduate school. I just…got busy. Or, you know, that's my story and I'm sticking to it." She huffed a humorless little laugh and couldn't quite keep her gaze locked with Gia's. "Pretty pathetic, huh?"

Gia scooted her chair closer and lifted Emie's chin with a gentle finger. "If you're pathetic, I'm pathetic, Em."

Emie blinked several times. "What do you mean?"

"I'm saying, I've done my share of dating, but I've never been in love, either."

"I don't believe it." She gaped.

Gia shrugged. "I have no reason to lie to you about it."

"But…but, why? Why haven't you fallen in love?" she sputtered. "There's no reason a woman like you—"

"There's that 'woman like you' stuff again." She shook her head, playfully stern. "You know what I'd like, Emie? If you could stop putting me in some mental category and just see *me*. Gia. For who I am, not who you think I should be."

Heat rose to her neck, and she almost hiccupped. God. God, Gia was right—Emie was a stereotyping jerk. "You're absolutely…I'm sorry. I don't mean it as an insult."

"I know, and it's okay. All I'm trying to tell you is, we all have our reasons for avoiding intimacy. You have yours, I have mine." Gia paused and sandwiched both of Emie's hands between her own, caressing the soft knuckles. "Stop thinking you're so different, *Profé*. Hardly anyone finds her true love in high school like Paloma did. I didn't and you didn't, and you know what? We're okay in my book."

Before Emie could delve into Gia's profound revelation, the sound of her front door opening broke the mood.

"Auntie Emie!" screamed Teddy from the front room.

Emie and Gia moved apart as tiny footsteps pummeled toward them. They shared a private smile when they heard Paloma hollering at the boys not to run in the house. Moments later, they found themselves wrapped in Pep's and Teddy's exuberant hugs.

A whirlwind of greetings, laughter, and exclamations of near-fatal hunger ensued. By the time Paloma had the boys settled around the table, the house was fragrant with the mingled scents of grilling steaks and savory side dishes. Emie had just poured herself and Gia a second glass of wine. She offered one to Paloma, as well, then poured milk for the boys. Gia put the finishing touches on the steaks and carried them to the cloth-draped table. Paloma led grace—something she was trying to teach the boys—then they began passing dishes.

"I'm not eatin' those," said Teddy. He stared with abject disgust at the bowl of glazed carrots before him. A recalcitrant cowlick stood up from his crown when he bent forward and scrunched his nose. "Betchtables make me sick."

"Yuck. I don't want 'em either," Pep added, stretching up from his seat of honor next to Gia to peer across the table into the serving bowl. His bruises had faded to nothing more than flat yellowish reminders of his problems.

"Teodoro, that's rude," Paloma scolded, her cheeks red with parental embarrassment. She glanced apologetically at Emie. "You'll eat what your auntie cooked, young man, or you'll go hungry." She fixed a death glare on her older son and flicked her hand toward the CorningWare. "Pep, I expect you to set the example for your brother. Now take some carrots."

Pep's small chin quivered with the horrific burden of having to set such an example. "Mama, please don't make me. They're *orange*."

"Actually, I didn't cook them," Emie cut in, hoping to aid Paloma in the battle. She smiled at the boys as she smoothed her napkin on her lap. "Gia did. They're glazed, which means they have butter and brown sugar on them."

"Did you really cook 'em, Gia?" Pep asked, his tone grave. He clearly disbelieved that the woman he'd come to revere would stoop so low as to cook the offensive items for dinner.

"I sure did."

"They're still betchtables no matter who cooked 'em,"

muttered Teddy, slumping back in his chair and pulling his feet up onto the seat.

"Feet down, young man."

Teddy did as he was told.

Paloma's eyes blazed. "You boys should be ashamed of yourselves acting like this. Apologize to Gia and Aunt Emie right now."

"So-o-orry," they groused with a distinct lack of sincerity.

"It's okay. Could you please—" Gia motioned for the bowl. Emie reached in front of Teddy and passed the carrots to Gia, who sneaked her a conspiratorial wink. "Thanks." She turned her attention to the boys' mother. "Carrots are superhero food, Paloma. I don't guess these guys are grown up enough to have any, which means, great—more for me. Mmm mmm mmm," she added, dishing up a large serving.

"Superhero food? Wha—? Oh. Right," Paloma said, catching on quickly after her moment of confusion. "I'd almost forgotten." Her eyes tracked Gia, unsure of the woman's next move but clearly willing to follow her lead.

Emie slanted a glance at the boys, who watched Gia with a rapturous combination of worship and horror. "But you didn't eat 'em when you were a kid, right, Gia?" Pep asked, in a please-don't-burst-my-bubble tone.

Gia raised her eyebrows while she finished chewing, then swallowed. "You kidding? I ate them all the time. Of course, I had special permission to eat superhero food because I wanted to grow up to have super powers." She flexed her arm, drawing every eye in the room to those toned, cut biceps.

Paloma gawked with unabashed approval, then stared pointedly at Emie, who only scowled in return. Pep's jaw dropped, and he peered into the carrot bowl with renewed interest. "What do they taste like?"

"You'll find out once you're old enough to try them." Gia popped a couple more carrots in her mouth, making yummy noises as she chewed.

Pep pondered this. "When's that?"

"You have to be at least ten, don't you think, Auntie?"

Emie bit her lip to hold back the smile and nodded. Gia Mendez was an absolute genius.

"I'm almost ten," Pep said, his gaze fixed longingly on the carrots. "I'm six, an' that's pretty close to ten."

"Mama, do you really hafta be ten to eat 'em?" Teddy stage whispered, his tone plaintive. "That's not fair, Pep's not ten."

"Not close enough, *chavalito*," Gia said to Pep, pretending not to have heard little Teddy. "Sorry."

Pep clicked his tongue and pouted.

Gia adjusted in her chair. "But I guess if you really want some, we can give you a couple on the sly."

The boy's face brightened. "For reals?"

Gia pretended to ruminate. She sucked in one side of her cheek and shook her head. "On second thought, I don't want to break the superhero rules."

"Aw, c'mon, Gia." Pep bounced. "No one'll know. Mama and Auntie Emie won't tell, will ya?"

They both shook their heads.

"Please?" came Teddy's piteous voice.

"You want some, too, little buddy?"

"Yeah," Teddy said, his eyes round. He sat on his hands.

Gia pulled a shocked face before glancing from Emie to Paloma. "What do you two think? Should we break the rules?"

Paloma couldn't speak; she covered her mouth with the side of her fist to hold in the laughter.

Emie cleared her throat. "Well, Teddy's four and Pep's six. If we add those together, that equals ten." She shrugged.

"I hadn't thought of that. Guess that's why you're the scientist, Em." Gia quirked her mouth to the side and toyed with the idea while the boys sat still as statues. When the tension was sufficiently high, she relented. "Okay. Just this once, you can have carrots."

"Yay!" Pep and Teddy cheered in stereo as Paloma dished

carrots up on their plates. She cast Gia a wry glance. "Woman, I don't know where you've been hiding yourself, but you are a G-O-D-D-E-S-S. I bow and scrape in your presence."

Gia laughed, jerking her chin toward the boys who were no longer paying attention to the conversation. "Naw, I was just a picky eater myself long ago. I know what it takes."

"Well, honey, you can eat with us any day."

Gia cut into her steak, then cast a glance at Emie. There was that "rescued by a gallant knight" look again.

The dinner had been a complete success. After Gia pulled the brilliant reverse-carrot-psychology trick on the boys, endearing herself to Paloma, she completely won Pep and Teddy over by taking them outside to sit in her much-coveted truck. She even revved the engine. She was the perfect guest and a wonderful friend. Emie liked her more now than she ever had.

Paloma had taken the kids home early, leaving Emie and Gia to share coffee on the back porch before calling it a night. The full moon cast a silvery glow over the yard, and a cool breeze swept over them. Emie closed her eyes and reveled in the near-perfect moment, wrapping her palms around her warm mug. "That was fun. It turned out good."

"I'll say. I'm stuffed," Gia said, patting her stomach. The lawn chair creaked as she adjusted her position. "I never should've had the second slice of chocolate cream pie."

Emie rolled her face toward Gia, feeling more relaxed in her company than she usually did. She liked being with her like this, without the makeover scheme or Elizalde or memories of the Barry Stillman fiasco getting in the way. "What's a little self-indulgence now and then?"

"True, but I'll never be able to sleep feeling like this." She grimaced. "Don't tell me you're one of those irritatingly self-controlled eaters who always leaves your last bite on the plate."

Emie laughed, deciding not to answer the playful question. "We could go for a walk, if you'd like. God knows I could use the exercise."

"Yeah? I'd love to." Gia stood, adjusting the waistband of her jeans as though they barely reached around her trim waist. "Let's do it before I burst."

After locking up the house, they meandered down the shadow-striped sidewalk talking about this and that, nothing important. They reached a particularly dark corner and Gia glanced around. "How safe is this neighborhood?"

"Relatively," she answered. "I wouldn't walk at night alone." She paused. "But I feel pretty safe with you."

Gia smiled and wound her arm around Emie's shoulders, pulling her closer. "You always say the right things, *querida*."

It didn't bother Emie one bit when Gia let her arm remain. "*I* always say the right things? What about that whole 'carrots are a superhero food' action you came up with? How brilliant was that? Did you see Pep and Teddy gobbling those vegetables?"

"Betchtables," Gia corrected her.

Emie chuckled.

"That was a good ploy, if I do say myself." Gia blew smugly on her fingernails and buffed them on the shoulder of Emie's shirt.

"I'll say." Emie reached up to adjust her phantom glasses, but stopped halfway and dropped her hand. She chuckled. "I can't get used to not having glasses on my face."

"You can always go back to wearing them."

She chose to ignore that rather than launch back into the "you look good in goggles" conversation. "I know you don't like me praising you, Gia, but I can't help it. Thank you for tonight, for showing the boys the truck, for just...everything."

"*De nada*. I like them. They're weird little creatures, children."

"I know. That's what makes them so fun." Emie peered up at Gia's profile. "How'd you get to be so good with kids?"

She shrugged. "I didn't know I was. Like I've said before, I haven't really been around them much. I suppose I just"—she paused, running a palm slowly down her own face—"remember growing up, how hard childhood was. I sympathize with them."

Emie navigated the cracked and buckled sidewalk, perplexed by this enigmatic woman's winsome words. She didn't understand. Her own childhood had been wonderful, her parents doting and supportive. But she wasn't so naïve as to believe everyone's youth had been idyllic. She wanted to push Gia to tell her what she'd meant, but didn't want to pry. They crossed the street and came upon the deserted elementary school campus.

"Is this Pep's school?"

"No. Deanne and Paloma don't live in this neighborhood." Emie studied the playground through the chain-link fence. The loose tetherball chains clanged and pinged against the poles, their song eerily desolate. Swings drifted gently, and tiny children's footprints still marred the sand at the bottom of the slide.

Childhood shouldn't be difficult.

That it might have been for Gia made Emie profoundly sad.

Before she could say anything, Gia grabbed her hand and pulled her toward the equipment. "Come on. It's been a long time since I've gone down the slide."

"Are you serious?"

Gia grinned. "Cut loose, Em. Last one to the slide is a rotten egg."

"No fair, I'm wearing sandals. You're wearing boots."

"Chicken!"

Emie's jaw dropped, and her inner child burst forth. "I know you are, but what am I?" She shoved Gia with all her might, taking advantage of her stumbling to launch into a full sprint. Gia took off after her, eventually passing her.

They paused at the slide, and she bent at the waist, sucking air. Gia did the same. "You cheated," Gia told her, laughing.

She pointed to her open toes. "I evened the field."

"And yet, I still won," Gia said smugly, her eyes smiling.

Emie snorted. "Oh, please. I let you win. Didn't want to damage your precious superhero ego."

Leaning her head back, Gia guffawed over that one. Their breathing back to normal, they ran from apparatus to apparatus laughing freely. Gia swung from the monkey bars while Emie tackled the slide. She got dizzy when Gia spun her on the merry-go-round, so they took a break and sat side by side on the swings. Emie let her feet dangle and drew shapes in the gravel with the toe of her sandal. She wondered again about Gia's upbringing and decided to broach the subject tactfully. "I bet you had a lot of fun as a kid."

Moonlight caught the side of Gia's face, illuminating the movement of her temple as she clenched her jaw. Finally, she looked at Emie. The chains of the swing were nestled in her crooked elbows, forearms crossed in front of her, each hand grasping the opposite chain. Slowly, she swiveled. "Emie...I should tell you something about myself."

Everything in Emie tensed. Gia's grave tone put her on guard. Was she an ex-con? Or married? *Or straight?* Yeah, that one was a little out there. She told herself to stop being ridiculous and let Gia talk. "O-okay. Go ahead."

Gia blew out a breath and stared off at the lonely monkey bars for a moment. Without looking at Emie, Gia said, "When I was growing up, I wasn't...a very nice person."

The mildness of the statement after all she'd suspected nearly caused Emie to laugh, but she didn't. The wary look on Gia's face told her this difficult confession clearly meant a lot to her. "What do you mean?"

Gia struggled to get the explanation out. "We all have roles as children...just like Pep and Teddy have theirs now. They shape us."

She inclined her head in agreement. "And your role was?"

Gia's eyes met hers directly, and the shame she saw in them made her stomach drop. "I was the bully," she choked out. "A pushy, cocky tough chick without a conscience or remorse. So filled with rage over whatever…I couldn't see straight. I was… no better than the boys beating up Pep."

The admission surprised Emie, and she didn't quite know what to say. She'd never met a gentler woman than Gia Mendez. She swallowed, measured her words. "G, small children are notoriously cruel to other kids." She bit her lip. "You know that, right?"

"It didn't end in childhood." Gia kicked up an arc of gravel. "I was cruel and bitter and mean until I turned eighteen. I was…a horrible person."

"Don't say that." Emie reached out and touched her leg, sensing Gia needed the contact. "The you I know is kind and—"

"No. Please. Don't give me credit where I don't deserve it, *querida*." Her body stiffened. "If it wasn't for one man, my art teacher, I'd probably be the same way today."

"But…but that's absurd."

Gia's face jerked up.

"You're giving this man way too much credit for the person you've become, Gia"—she held up a palm—"and I don't mean to downplay how much he contributed to your personal growth. We all have mentors and guides along the path. But does he control you? Are you his puppet?"

"N-no, but—"

She leaned in and took Gia's hand. "Honey, people change. They transform." She paused to swallow thickly, realizing she'd just called Gia *honey*. True, she called her best friends *honey* all the time, but this felt different. She forged ahead before Gia could deny her words. "Anyone who knows you now can see what a good, gentle person you are." A pause. "Then again, yeah, I guess you could say you're still a bully."

"W-what?"

Emie nodded. "It's true. Except the only person you're beating up now is yourself. And you don't deserve it, G. Not one bit."

The moment stilled so profoundly, even the tetherball

chains fell silent. Gia stared at her, a myriad of emotions crossing the smooth curves and angles of her face—wonder, disbelief, gratitude, relief.

Emie had never felt so close to another person. She reached out and smoothed her palm down Gia's cheek. "You can't base your adult self-image on the child or teen you may have been. Angry or not."

Gia's throat tightened. "I could say the same to you."

Emie sat back and blinked. "Meaning what?"

A long pause uncoiled. "Who convinced you, Em, that you weren't worthy of love?"

Emie scoffed, raising her eyebrows and looking toward the moon. "Ah, you mean other than Vitoria Elizalde, Barry Stillman, and two hundred live audience viewers bearing signs?"

Gia shook her head once, not backing down. "That's surface stuff, nothing you deserved. You had to have already believed it for it to have hurt you so badly."

Emie's eyes traced Gia's face for a moment before she sighed and leaned her cheek against the chain of her swing. "No one told me that exactly, but I overheard something, and yeah, I guess it did guide my life choices. I've never pursued a relationship, focusing instead on my career."

"What did you hear? Who said it?"

"My Tía Luz." To her abject horror, tears rose to her eyes and one rolled down her cheek. Just like that, Gia Mendez had cracked her protective shell.

"What happened? Tell me."

She regaled the awful story, unmindful of the fact that the first tear's faithful followers began to plink-plunk on her lap. When she finished, Gia reached out and cupped her chin. Emie sniffed, but didn't meet her gaze.

"Look at me, Emie. Please."

She did. Grudgingly.

"Baby, if you could see yourself through my eyes, you'd know how beautiful you are. How amazing." Gia's voice whispered, caressed. "When will you listen to your best friends who think so highly of you? Ah, Em, you more than grew into the superficiality of your looks. You grew into the total package."

Emie sniffled again, feeling somehow secure with Gia. It didn't scare her to say what she felt. "I don't know about that, but y-you make me feel good about myself."

"Yeah?" A sad smile lifted one corner of Gia's mouth. She wicked a tear off Emie's cheek. "Then my life is complete."

Emie's heart expanded, and she pressed her face into Gia's warm palm. "Now you tell me, Gia Mendez," she asked in a tremulous voice, "was that the statement of a bully?"

A silence ensued, after which Gia grabbed the chains of Emie's swing and pulled her closer. She trapped Emie with her legs and wrapped strong arms around her, holding her in an odd suspended embrace. The bolts above them creaked as the breeze swayed them, and the rest of the world faded into nonexistence. "Don't speak, *querida*," Gia told Emie when her lips parted. "I'm locking away this moment in my heart."

CHAPTER SEVEN

G ia stepped back from the easel, assessing the wet canvas with a critical eye. The mood was perfect now, the changes she'd made exactly what the piece had been lacking. Pleasure surged through her. A glance at her watch told her it was almost time to meet Emie. She stuffed rags into the prized, paint-spattered coffee can she'd inherited from Mr. Fuentes and capped it. The familiar odors of linseed oil and viscous paints tickled her senses.

Red sable brushes and palette knives lay scattered like pick-up sticks across her work table. With a frown, she began to gather them. She wasn't usually this haphazard, but she'd been so excited over finally figuring out what was lacking in the painting, she'd wanted to get the brainstorm from her imagination to the canvas as quickly as possible. She'd gotten the major work done, and the finishing touches could wait until after their trip to the mall.

Careful not to drip too much paint, Gia traversed the drop cloth–shrouded hardwood floor, then dunked the tools in Mason jars of turps she'd lined up on the small kitchen counter. The pungent, almost spicy chemical scent permeated the room.

She'd known where she wanted to go with this painting from her first charcoal sketch, but something had been off. Try as she might, she hadn't been able to breathe life into it. *Until now*.

Wiping her hands on the tattered apron she wore, Gia turned back to the portrait of Emie and smiled.

Yes.

The eyes had been wrong before, she just hadn't pinpointed it until last night while sitting on the swings. They'd shared so much of themselves beneath the harvest moon, Gia felt like she'd really seen Emie for the first time. Had seen *into* her. And when Emie had looked at her that certain way…breathtaking.

She'd added a luminescence to the portrait's eyes, a deepness to the expression, until looking at it felt like…coming home. It was sure to draw the attention of the gallery owners. Even if they weren't turned on by the portrait, Gia hoped Emie would love it. More than anything, Gia wanted Emie to see herself with a fresh perspective—Gia's. Maybe then Emie would recognize the power of her own feminine power. Maybe then the psychic wounds of Tía Luz's unthinking words, of Vitoria Elizalde's careless arrogance, of *The Barry Stillman Show*'s cruelty, would heal.

Gia cleaned her marble palette, then quickly tossed the crinkled paint tubes she'd used into a large Tupperware container, noticing she was low on Titanium White and Viridian Green. As she stowed the plastic tub in the refrigerator, she made a mental note to ask Emie if she minded stopping by an art supply store while they were out. She'd pick up a few fresh linen canvases, extra stretcher bars, more gesso, and a spare drop cloth while she was at it. She'd need the stock, as a multitude of new ideas had begun to whirl through her brain. She couldn't believe how inspired she'd been since she moved here. Everything about Emie stoked her creative fire.

Clock check. Time was running out. Yanking the apron, then the T-shirt over her head, Gia stood at the sink and scrubbed paint from her hands and arms with Lava soap, then headed for the shower. She needed to call and confirm her appointment with the gallery owner, but it would have to wait. If last night with Emie was any indication, they were headed in a very intriguing direction. Gia didn't want to miss one single moment she could spend with the lovely professor.

❖

"Meow?" Emie gaped in disbelief at the tiny letters printed on the bottom of the twenty-five-dollar lipstick tube. For one, she couldn't believe they charged twenty-five smackers for something so small and frivolous in the whole scheme of life, but more importantly, "What the hell kind of color is 'Meow'?"

Gia moved around the glass counter and took the lipstick. She uncapped it and checked, then replaced the cap and handed it back. Her eyes sparkled with mirth. "It's, uh, red."

Emie scoffed, planting one fist on her hip. "So why not call it red? What pretentious idiot came up with 'Meow' as a color name?" A distant part of her brain registered admiration that Gia—a woman who didn't seem to use any of these products—had no ego issues shopping for cosmetics. Even so, Emie couldn't get past the fact that some retro Cro-Magnon jerk had named a women's product something so base-level offensive. *Meow*, of all things. "My feminist core feels like it should be outraged by the implication."

Gia chuckled, giving her a patronizing little pat on the shoulder. "Well, we're staying away from true reds for you anyway, so pull in your claws, Miss Kitty."

A monosyllable of disbelief escaped from her throat as she stared at Gia. One corner of her mouth, then the other quivered into a smile against her will. "Gia Mendez, please tell me you did *not* just say what I thought you said."

"Okay, I didn't." She lifted her hands to resemble claws and made a cat-fighting noise that sounded something like, "Reeowr!"

"Oh-ho-*ho*, you are treading on dangerous ground, woman." Emie set the gleaming black tube on the counter with lighthearted disgust and smacked Gia in her solid abs with the back of one hand. The shopping excursion had been enjoyable so far, their friendship having reached a higher plane. Gia seemed more comfortable with her, and Emie felt the same. Just being around

Gia boosted her mood. "Miss Kitty," she sputtered. "Jerk. I ought to—"

"I'm only teasing you." Gia hooked an arm around her neck and pulled her playfully closer as they ambled down the department store aisle toward the next cosmetic counter. "Start looking for a nice, nonthreatening shade in the burgundy or wine family, *querida*. With your new hair tint, I'd like to stay with that color palette. Think your feminist core can handle that?" Gia asked, breath against Emie's temple before releasing her.

Emie's stomach fluttered when Gia pulled away, but in a wholeheartedly good way. In fact, she was in better spirits than she'd been in...forever. If nothing more, after the previous evening, she knew she and Gia shared a special friendship no one could ever breach. They'd confided their deepest pains in each other, and she'd gotten the impression Gia had never opened up to anyone else in such a way. But she'd trusted Emie enough to share it with her, which meant they truly were friends in the best sense of the word. She'd take that if she couldn't have all of her. Body, mind, soul.

Despite her warm, fuzzy feelings, Emie scowled at Gia for good measure. "Don't change the subject. I'll get you for the Miss Kitty comment. Setting us back to the 1950s, I swear. When you least expect it, watch out."

"I'm shaking in my boots." Gia rolled her eyes.

A beautiful plum-colored silk and satin cocktail dress in the adjacent department caught Emie's eye, and she approached it, reaching out to run the sensuous fabric through her fingers. The bias cut made the dress drape the mannequin in a subtly sexy way, and the brief hemline lifted it out of the ordinary category. It was exquisite. Powerfully feminine. Exactly the kind of dress Emie always wished she were daring enough to wear.

"Hey, we're shopping for cosmetics. Remember?" Gia came up beside her and shot a brief glance at the dress.

"Sorry. I was just..." She lifted the hem once again then let the fabric drop and turned. "I'm sorry, where do you need me?"

Gia gestured to a chrome and white vinyl stool next to a pristine cosmetic display. The backlit sign boasted the line's gentleness to sensitive skin. "Have a seat here. Enough jacking around. I'm going to ask the rep if she'll let me test some of the products on you."

Emie wiggled into the stool, hooking her low heels over the rung near the bottom of the chrome legs. An absurd muzak version of Will Smith's "Gettin' Jiggy Wit It" piped through the air. All around her, shoppers eagerly handed over their hard-earned cash for the privilege of taking home promises of beauty and better sex disguised as overpriced tubes of lipstick and concealer.

Glancing around at the various cosmetic reps, Emie came to the disturbing conclusion that she wouldn't want a makeup job like any one of these purported experts. She understood they were in the business, but many of them looked like they'd applied colors with a putty knife beneath bad lighting. A clear case of oversell. Emie watched with amusement as shoppers walked in a wide arc around an overzealous perfume demonstrator, then set her wallet on the counter with a clunk.

Her eyes sought and found Gia crossing toward an adjacent cosmetic display. Gia raised a hand and caught the attention of a white-jacketed aesthetician with come-hither eyes and a propensity for leading with her pelvis as she walked. Or perhaps it was only because she undulated toward Gia that her pelvis ran point man for the rest of her body, Emie couldn't be sure.

When the woman's swishing hips reached Gia, she stopped, her smile lending a whole new layer to the concept of customer service. While Gia explained and gestured, the woman batted her lashes and nodded. She leaned closer than necessary when Gia extracted some document from her wallet for the woman to inspect. After studying the item, the woman thrust out a hipbone and glanced toward Emie, her cool assessment and blatant envy zinging like an electrical bolt.

In an uncharacteristic move, Emie squared her shoulders and bestowed a bet-you-wish-YOU-were-with-her smile on the makeup schlepper. Her misplaced bravado both cheered and jolted her. Yikes, when had she gotten so catty? Could Gia's Miss Kitty comment have a basis in fact? *Reeowr!* The thought made her laugh.

With Ms. Pelvis gyrating alongside, Gia approached. "What's so funny, Em?" Gia asked.

"Ah, nothing. Just sitting here amusing myself." Emie smiled at the woman, this time genuinely. She reached up and patted her own face. "So, any hope for this?"

Ms. Pelvis, whose real name according to the rectangular silver tag on her jacket was Inga, beamed back. "Of course." She snaked a hand tipped with Meow-colored claws around Gia's biceps and squeezed ever so slightly. "I'm going to set up our makeover tray and give Gia, here, free rein. Since she's a licensed professional and all." *Bat, bat.*

"Fabulous," Emie replied, surprisingly entertained by it all. She was completely out of her element but didn't feel the slightest bit intimidated by it. She glanced at Gia and gave a few strategic *bat-bats* herself. Gia's brows furrowed in confusion, but she managed a private little smile.

Inga rounded to the business side of the counter, gushing and fawning while she laid out the accouterments of beauty making. Gia made polite conversation but didn't succumb to Inga's coquettish banter, a fact that raised Gia immeasurably in Emie's esteem. After lingering longer than necessary, Inga swished reluctantly away and Gia got to work.

Emie dismissed the urge to quip about Inga's flagrant flirting. Instead, she closed her eyes and lost herself in the feeling of Gia smoothing moisturizer on her skin with those soft, warm fingers. She imagined them smoothing over other parts of her body, teasing her nipples.

Entering her.

Emie groaned.

"What's wrong?"

Oops. "Uh, nothing. Sorry." Her mind wandered back to the playground and a smile lifted her lips.

"Okay, 'fess up. What are you thinking?" Gia asked.

"Nothing." She paused. "Well, actually, I was thinking about last night. I had a great time. Thank you."

"Don't thank me. I enjoyed it, too."

"I'm glad we talked, Gia," she said in a private tone.

Gia's hands stopped moving, and she flipped her fingers over to caress Emie's cheek with the backs of them. "Me, too."

They shared a lingering glance that plunged Emie's stomach. Tremulously, she said, "Don't let me interrupt what you were doing. It feels good. You touching me, I mean." Her eyes drifted shut, unable to face the boldness of her own comment.

"It does, huh?"

"Gia," Emie said, in a playful warning tone.

Gia laughed softly, then continued her work. "I'm not going to do a full face here," she said. "I just want to test some colors and make sure your skin doesn't react to anything, then we'll take the products home."

"Thief," Emie teased.

Gia scoffed, grabbing a white foam triangle from the tray to dab at her face. "Oh, believe me, no law breaking involved. You'll be whipping out your platinum card before we hit the road." She lifted Emie's chin and tickled her lips with the sponge.

Emie squinted one eye open. "On that note, any chance you can try to select a lipstick that *isn't* twenty-five bucks?"

"I'll try," Gia said wryly, continuing to touch her face. "But I have this thing about quality products, so beware."

Emie reached up and grabbed Gia's wrist, narrowing her eyes in what she hoped was a threatening, all-business look. "You might have champagne taste, woman, but I've got a beer budget, so frugality is the key."

"Yeah, yeah." Gia grinned. "Close your eye before we irritate your contact lenses."

Emie obeyed.

A few muzak-laden moments passed before Gia murmured, "You have really good bones."

"Said the undertaker to the cadaver," Emie replied.

Gia groaned. "You know what I mean. Bone *structure*. Nice high cheekbones, a good forehead."

Emie's eyes popped open and she gripped the edge of the vinyl seat. An unfamiliar feeling of pride rose in her chest. "Really?"

"Really."

She studied Gia's face. "No one's ever said anything like that to me before."

"Does that mean I get points for originality?"

"God, G. You have enough points, trust me."

"Is that so?" Her brows arched. She held swabs of different-colored foundation next to her cheek and neck, turning her face this way and that. She chose one, applied it with her fingers and a sponge, then selected a matching powder. Picking up a huge brush that looked like a guinea pig on a stick, she said, "Keep your eyes closed tight while I powder you."

Emie complied, but halfway through the process, an unsettling thought popped into her head. "We don't have much time before the faculty get-together. I don't feel like we've made much progress with my new look. Puh! Puh!" Grimacing, she blew powder off her lips, reaching up to smear the back of her hand across her mouth and swipe particles from her teeth. "Yuck."

Gia laughed. "Makeup artists' rule number one. Don't open your mouth when you're getting powdered."

"Sorry. You're forgetting—low-maintenance woman, here. I'm new to this." Emie watched Gia's hand hover over a lovely pale blusher before she selected a darker shade that reminded her of Pep's purple bruises. Great. A needle of anxiety pricked at Emie.

"Then I'm sorry, too." Gia plucked a brush from a clear Lucite holder. "I'll keep you more apprised of what I'm doing."

Emie crossed her legs and sat back in the chair. "Start by explaining how we can possibly transform me from dull to 'eat your heart out, Vitoria' in the few days we have left."

"Don't worry, *querida*, we have plenty of time." She dipped the glossy brush in the cheek color, tapped off the excess, then tested it on Emie's face. After studying the color from the front and side, Gia nodded, then wiped the color off with a tissue. The bruise blusher went into the to-buy pile, much to Emie's chagrin. "It's just a makeover, you know. Cosmetics. Not plastic surgery."

"Uh-huh." Emie eyed the stack of products she was doomed to purchase. Assessing each one the random value of twenty-five bucks, she figured she was a couple hundred dollars in the hole so far, not counting tax. "What else do we need to do?"

"We'll buy all this and hair products today and look for an outfit tomorrow." Gia paused, sifting through a cup of pencils. "By the way, do you mind if we swing by an art store on the way home? I'm low on supplies." She plunked a tube of raccoon-black mascara and a grape eyeliner stick in the purchase stack.

Ka-ching! Emie swallowed. "Of course not. Whatever you need." In went an eyebrow pencil, a pack of makeup brushes, and a lip-liner that reminded Emie of the Razzmatazz crayon in Teddy's Crayola 96-count Big Box. Gia topped it with a bag of foam triangles. Emie pointed. "Um, I hate to spoil your vicarious spree, but I'm not independently wealthy, you know. I'm in higher ed. We go to school for, oh, about a decade just to be underpaid."

"Don't worry. I'm only getting the basics." Gia smirked.

"*This* is how you'd define 'the basics'? How do women afford to keep themselves up?" Emie couldn't help but think Gia was enjoying the heck out of her fiscal discomfiture.

Gia skirted around the money vein. "I was thinking we'd do

a trial run of the hair and makeup this evening, just to make sure we have everything we need before the big event." She slanted Emie a wary glance. "We'll make a night of it. Maybe we can order in Chinese, if you'd like."

"Okay." Emie didn't care. Right now, she eyed the product mound. "Is that all? Please say yes."

"Nope. We still have to get the most important thing."

"What's that, an offshore account to pay for it all?"

Gia leveled her with an "I'm being patient, here" stare. "The lipstick, *querida*. Nothing sexier on a woman than a bright, pouty, kissable mouth."

"How could I forget?" Emie grabbed Gia's arm, trying not to be distracted by how good the muscles felt beneath her velvety soft skin. "Please don't pick a lipstick called Meow or anything equally repulsive."

"Emie?"

"Yes?"

Gia chucked Emie's chin with a knuckle and shook her head slowly. "Are you always this bossy?"

She sniffed. "I just know what I *don't* like. And I don't like cosmetics with names that objectify women."

"Understood." Gia picked up a gold-tubed lipstick, uncapped it, and smiled. "Here we go. Perfect. And it's called"—she flipped it over and read the tiny label—"Midnight Bordeaux. Can you handle that?"

Emie reached for the gleaming case and peered inside. Her jaw dropped. "Bordeaux? It's *black*!"

"Deep wine," Gia countered.

She double-checked. "No, black. Pitch-black. Geez. Midnight Bordello would be a more accurate name for this horrific color." Jab, jab went the anxiety needle, drawing blood this time. "You can't possibly think that'll look good on me."

"Of course it will. I'm an expert, remember?" She took the lipstick back and added it to the tally.

"Wait." Panic mounted in Emie's chest. "There's no talking you out of that lipstick?"

"Nope. It's dramatic. It makes a statement."

"Yeah—I'm a terrier—I have black lips." Emie extracted her credit card from her wallet. "That's the statement. Not my idea of a great fashion—"

"Emie, a little trust?" Gia chuckled. "I'm good, but I can't pull off a cat joke and a dog joke in the same shopping trip."

Emie jammed her arms crossed and glared at the offending lipstick. "I am so not amused by you right now."

"Well, it's nice to see you've got the pout down pat." Gia scooped the pile of cosmetics against her chest and smiled. "Come on, *Profé*. You'll get over it." She held out a palm for Emie's credit card. "Let's go max out your plastic, baby."

❖

"What do you use that for?" Emie asked, pointing at the gesso Gia held while they waited for the clerk to bring out the canvases. Customers swarmed through the art supply store, and though the employees seemed attentive, there were only so many of them to go around.

"This?" She clunked it on the counter. "It is applied to ground the bare canvas. Prepare it for the paint," she added, when Emie's quizzical frown said she didn't quite get it.

"Oh, I didn't know you had to do that," she said, chagrined. "I figured you just kind of…slapped the paint on when you had a creative brainstorm. I'm afraid I don't know much about your profession. But I'd love to learn more."

"Some artists coat the canvas with rabbit skin glue before the gesso," she told her, "but a lot of curators frown on that practice anymore." She leaned in and lowered her tone. "Critters think rabbit skin glue is a delicacy."

"Ah…yeah. Gross." Her nose crinkled at the thought. She

waited patiently until the clerk had handed Gia the canvases and a few tubes of paint. As they walked to the cash register, Emie said, "Tell me more about oil painting."

"Oh, you know, it's pretty much slapping paint on a canvas whenever a creative brainstorm hits. I'm tired of talking about me. Tell me about *your* job."

Emie's face came up, surprised. "Really? No one ever wants to talk about what I do."

"Why? Cloning is much more interesting than painting."

She laughed, and they piled the goods on the checkout counter. "Well, what do you want to know?"

Gia spread her arms in a gesture of helplessness. "I don't even know enough about it to ask a proper question. I just keep thinking about evil duplicates of people storming the planet and wreaking havoc."

She rolled her eyes. "Jesus, Hollywood. The bane of my existence." A gum-popping clerk began listlessly ringing up their purchases. She wore the vacant stare of a disillusioned minimum-wage earner. "We're working on the medical advances human cloning may provide rather than on the sci-fi aspect."

"Like what?" Gia extracted a credit card from her wallet and handed it to the checker after the girl monotoned the total to no one in particular.

"Well, hmm. There's so much." Emie pondered it, then flipped her hand over. "One example would be the possibility of being able to clone a heart disease sufferer's healthy heart cells and then inject them into the damaged areas. We do a lot of studies with embryonic stem cells, too."

"Which means what? In plain English, please. Or Spanish," Gia added, with a smile.

Emie crossed her arms and leaned one hip against the counter. "We're researching whether stem cells can be grown in order to produce organs or tissues to repair or replace damaged ones. Skin cells for burn victims, spinal cord cells for people with quadriplegia. Like that. If the tissues were cloned from the patient rather than donated, the rejection rate would plummet."

Gia grabbed her bags absentmindedly, engrossed in the topic. "And that's cloning? I never knew. How do you grow these cells?"

Emie pressed her lips together and considered the question as they walked out to the truck, then tried to explain the procedure in as nontechnical terms as possible. She knew the scientific babble was what put most people off.

Gia slammed the tailgate and wiped her palms together to brush off the road dust. "So, as long as the technology isn't banned by people who think it's all a science-fiction ploy to take over the world, a lot of diseases and conditions could benefit from cloning."

Emie nodded, as always energized by the topic that had fired her blood since high school. "Potentially. A lot more research needs to be done but it's exciting." She shrugged. "Problem is, we need grant monies and governmental support, which is difficult to secure when seemingly every special interest group in the world protests the research. They just don't understand the potential."

"What wonderful and fulfilling work you do."

She sighed. "I love my career, but it has its negative aspects. You know, I'm the only woman on the research team—not counting that bitch, Vitoria—and I'm also the only person under the age of forty. Combine that with being a quote-unquote minority and I'm quite the oddity."

"You should be proud."

"I am. Don't get me wrong. It's just burdensome sometimes to be the frontrunner. The token Latina, some people think. I must be there because of a quota, not my brains." She huffed. "I've worked goddamned hard to get where I am, ever since I first learned about human cloning in my high school genetics class."

"I'm sure you have. I wouldn't imagine anything less."

Emie bestowed a smile of pure gratitude. "Not to mention, the field is packed with arrogant, prima donna men—and women—who puff up their chests at the thought of a thirty-year-old woman working on a level commensurate with their own."

Like Elizalde, Gia thought. That Emie showed even the slightest interest in the woman completely baffled Gia. And rankled her. She didn't want to think about it.

"If we had more kind, intelligent scientists in the field, I'd probably be much happier. People like you," Emie added quietly.

Gia warmed at the compliment and averted her gaze. And here she'd been thinking Emie would be bored hanging out with a simple painter. Maybe she'd been wrong. God, she wanted to hold Emie's body against her own. Emie made her feel so incredible, so special and…gentle. *Gentle* had never been in her repertoire. Her swelling emotions warned her to get back on track, and quick. "What about things like injured joints or amputated limbs?" She held her door open while Emie climbed into the truck. "Could cloning possibly regenerate those for a person?"

Emie's face brightened. "Exactly! Wow, it's so wonderful to talk to someone who just gets it. *That*"—she poked her finger softly into Gia's upper chest—"is the type of human cloning research we do. We're not out to recreate emotionless human duplicates."

Gia raised her hands like a heavyweight who'd just won the world title. "And Mendez chalks up another point for catching on. The crowd goes crazy." She cupped her hands around her mouth and imitated crowd cheering noises. It was a feeble attempt to lighten what had morphed into an intimate mood before she gave in to the impulse to gather Emie against her chest and rain kisses on her face, her neck.

Lower.

Emie shook her head and laughed a little, then studied Gia intently. "Ever thought about going into the sciences, G? You've obviously got the mind for it."

Gia pulled a skeptical face but pleasure from the compliment swirled through her. "No chance of that. I'll leave the hard work to experts like you. I'm perfectly happy painting."

"Which is a perfectly brilliant contribution to the world."

Time stilled.

Attraction crackled.

"Ah, sweet Emie." Gia caressed Emie's arm slowly from shoulder to wrist. "A woman sure could get used to being around you."

❖

Later that evening, Emie perched on the edge of the bathroom vanity while Gia applied the promised "full face." She hadn't seen it or her hair. But based on what she could feel, spiky quite literally described the hairstyle. It felt crunchy, sharp enough to put a freaking eye out. She could only wonder what effect the glitter spray had on the whole look, God help her.

"Quit smashing your spikes."

"Sorry. It feels funny." She folded her nervous hands in her lap. An idea struck. "You getting hungry yet? We could take a break and order dinner." She really just wanted an excuse to turn around and get a sneak preview of her face.

"No, you can't peek, but nice try." Gia glared. "We're almost done. And in answer to your question, I can wait to order unless you're going to die of starvation."

"I can wait, too," she muttered, grumpy that Gia had pegged her amateurish ploy.

Gia had been firing off questions about her job since the minute she walked in the door, which pleased Emie. Most women she'd encountered had either been bored by the topic or intimidated by her expertise. Gia seemed genuinely interested.

As though reading Emie's thoughts, Gia deftly turned the conversation back to the topic. "How does that bitch, Elizalde, fit into the research team?"

Oddly enough, thinking of Elizalde didn't infuriate Emie as much as it had right after the *Stillman Show* disaster. She found the woman rather…pathetic. Though she still wanted to get her back for what she'd done. "She's on a two-year faculty exchange from Universidade Federal de São Paulo," Emie said. "She's actually a medical doctor and she's part of the embryonic stem cell project. Hot stuff in her country. In the whole field, really."

"Hmm," Gia said, sounding unimpressed. "Stare at my throat and don't blink." Gia applied mascara to her lashes in silence. When she finished, she stuck the wand back into the tube and cast Emie a sidelong glance. "Can I ask you a question that's none of my business?"

"Great opening. Really sets a person's mind at ease." She gave Gia a droll smile. "But sure. Go ahead."

"What do you see in that woman?"

Emie's forehead crinkled. "Vitoria?"

Gia turned her back and took a moment to rifle through Emie's new cache of expensive cosmetics. "Yeah," she said through clenched teeth.

Emie shrugged, confused. "Well…I don't know what you mean. I respect her work, her contribution to the field of genetic research…and we're lucky to have her on the project."

"But is that enough of a reason—" The ringing phone interrupted Gia's question.

"I should get that." Yes! Now was her chance to catch a glimpse of her makeup. "Fine, but *no peeking*."

"Okay," she fibbed, jumping off the counter. She *had* to see it so she could control her reaction in case she hated the way it looked. Not that she was a pessimist. "I'll run downstairs and order the food while I'm at it. It will be at least forty-five minutes before they deliver."

Gia held up a finger. "I'm serious, Em, don't look."

Emie ignored the warning, pounding her way down the stairs to snag up the phone on the fourth ring. "Hello?"

"Hey, chickie."

"Iris! We haven't talked in forever." Slowly, with trepidation squeezing her lungs and horror flick background music playing in her head, Emie turned in measured increments to face the hall mirror. She cajoled herself:

Maybe it wouldn't be so bad.

Maybe Gia decided to go for subtlety.

Maybe—

The first glimpse was like a punch in the gut.

Dumbstruck, she sucked in a breath. The only thing that could make her look more gruesome was the addition of black lipstick, *which came next.* "Oh. My. Fucking. God."

"What's wrong, Em? Don't say that in front of your mother, by the way."

"This can't happen. You have to see this," Emie rasped. She wadded the bottom of her shirt in her fist and glanced behind her to make sure Gia wasn't within earshot.

"Why are you whispering? See what?"

Panicked, she searched her brain for a feasible escape route from this nightmarish makeover plan. Sleazy was one thing, but she never expected it to be this macabre. Somehow she had to convince Gia this wasn't the way she should look. An idea struck her. "Are you busy?"

"No, that's why I called." Iris sounded mystified. "I thought I'd stop by and chat later if you're free."

Emie licked her lips, her head bouncing like a frenzied dashboard Chihuahua. "Good. Yes. Excellent. Holy, holy *shit.* Come soon. Come *now.*"

"Emie Jaramillo, you're jabbering. What is going on?"

She sucked a breath and blurted it all in one jumbled exhale. "Gia did my makeup and hair, kind of a dress—" *hiccup* "—rehearsal for Friday's party. Anyway, do you remember that old Cher song, 'Gypsies, Tramps, and Thieves'?"

"Yeah."

"Well, right now I look like all three of them rolled into

one ridiculous—" *hiccup* "—caricature. Mixed in with a little science-fiction glitter for good measure." The description was an understatement. No way could she show her face in public looking like this. She glanced into the mirror at the unrecognizable hooker-slash-vampire staring back at her. Her stomach cramped. She fought back a whimper.

"Uh-oh. You're hiccupping. It can't be good."

"It isn't!" she half gasped, half slurred.

"Okay, wait," said Iris, ever the voice of rationality. "Did you somehow give Gia the impression it was a costume party?"

"No, of course not." Panic bubbled inside Emie. She bounced, shaking her hand with urgency. "Stop asking stupid questions and come—" *hiccup* "—over. You have to convince Gia this looks ridiculous. Maybe if she hears it from you, considering you're—"

"All right, all right," Iris soothed, sounding apprehensive. "But what if you're wrong and I like it?"

"Trust me." Her throat clenched. "You'll *hate* it."

A sigh. "I'm on my way."

Emie hung up and ordered their food, adding an order of Kung Pao chicken—Iris's favorite—in case she hadn't eaten. She took the sympathetic restauranteur's suggestion to order her sesame beef extra hot because the chile supposedly cured hiccups. After arranging her expression in a semblance of casual innocence, she pressed a palm to her trembling torso and headed up the stairs to meet her black-lipped fate.

In the bathroom, Gia blocked the mirror. She cupped a hand next to Emie's face like a horse blinder while she got resituated on the sink. "You didn't look, did you?"

How could she lie without flat-out lying? "I, um, caught a glimpse in the hall mirror but—" *hiccup* "—didn't get a close look." She changed the subject before Gia had a chance to dig deeper. "Iris's going to join us for dinner, do you mind?"

"Of course not. We're almost done here." Gia's gold-flecked eyes narrowed in suspicion. "Why do you have the hiccups?"

"M-medically, I think it's when you swallow air."

"That's a belch."

"Whatever." Emie licked her lips. "Let's finish before she gets here. What do we have left? Just the terrier lips?"

Gia flattened her mouth into a line and chastised Emie with a glance. "Just the lip color, yes."

She rummaged out a tiny brush and began to blacken it with the offending lip gunk. Emie watched with mounting stress. Did Gia really like this look?

"So, a hint." She posed gracefully. "H-how do I—" *hiccup* "—look?"

Gia stood back and grabbed Emie's chin, turning her head this way and that, studying her. "Definitely exotic."

Emie blurted a nervous laugh. Her palms were sweaty. "Well, good, that's what we wanted." She toyed with the flyer that had come in the lipstick box while Gia held her chin and painted the funereal shade on her mouth. Finished, Gia grinned, then began gathering the products. Emie focused on reading the lipstick flyer, which listed instructions and marketing claims in English, German, French, Spanish, and an Asian language she didn't recognize. Who'd need instructions for lipstick? she wondered. "Can I look now?" she asked.

"Not yet. Let me, first." Gia breached her personal space and scrutinized her up close. "You look great, Em."

Was the woman delusional? Emie's eyes read faster. "Oh, thanks."

Gia's knuckles moved to rest on either side of Emie's hips, effectively trapping her in place. Her musky female scent, like warm vanilla and hot sex, surrounded Emie. Something moved between them with the power of the earth's tectonic plates shifting. *Oh, God.*

"I personally think you always look great."

Uh-huh. Sure you do.

"But this is good, too," Gia murmured.

"Are you sure?" Emie tensed, inadvertently squeezing Gia's

hips with her thighs. Those sexy eyes smoldered, and Gia moved closer until their faces were mere inches apart. The end of Gia's ponytail fell over her shoulder.

Hijola, Gia was going to kiss her.

Emie knew it, could feel it like a déjà vu, like it had already happened and she was reliving it in Technicolor and surround sound. They'd just managed to get their friendship on track. Gia couldn't possibly kiss her.

God, please kiss me.

Her tongue seemed to vibrate with desire, to tingle with the need to taste this woman. Unable to stop herself, she raked her newly blackened lips through her teeth.

Gia's gaze dropped. Smoldered. "Hey, now," she drawled. "You're going to chew all that lipstick off, *querida*."

Emie held up the accordioned product flyer. "Uh, it's chew-proof, according to"—she held her breath and staved off a hiccup—"this. Though I'm sure they didn't do a scientific study to prove such a claim." Wow. And she'd always thought the concept of a person's heart being *in* her throat was metaphorical. She swallowed—barely.

"Know what else it says, Em? That it's kiss-proof."

An airless chuckle strangled past the heart that was blocking her normal throat function. "Definitely no scientific studies to prove that one, I'd bet."

Gia's gaze rested on her mouth. Emie could see the pulse in the side of Gia's long, sexy neck, could feel her warm breath tickle her lips. "Probably not," Gia murmured, moving closer… closer still, "but, baby, there's definitely something to be said for testimonial evidence."

CHAPTER EIGHT

Emie reached out intending to press against Gia's chest and prevent the kiss, but her brain had other plans. Before she could stop herself, she had gathered a fistful of Gia's shirt and pulled her roughly closer. Their mouths came together with a passion so innate it was inevitable. A moan tore from Emie's throat, or maybe Gia's. Emie couldn't tell which, but the sound was guttural and spontaneous. Surprised, yet…not. A promise.

Gia's warm sugar tongue eagerly explored her mouth, and goddamn, the woman could kiss. Emie's hands snaked around to Gia's nape, releasing the ponytail from its rubber-band confines. She'd been wanting to do that for a long time. She drove her fingers into Gia's shiny hair and scrunched it in her fists, indulging herself in the silk of Gia. The position raised her breasts to meet Gia's, and she pressed closer, knowing nothing beyond her blinding need to rub their softness together, to seek the hard points of Gia's nipples with her own. Everything within her throbbed, opened, wet and hot. Her libido switched her brain on autopilot and released her to the wild, sensual ride.

Gia's mouth lifted, but not too far. "Sweet God, *querida*, I want—"

"I know." The words shook with wonder and surprise.

Gia palmed Emie's hips and pulled her closer until the insides of her thighs made contact with Gia's hipbones, until nothing separated them besides denim and desire, a few scraps of clothing and moist, familiar heat. Gia captured Emie's mouth again. She traced Emie's lips with her warm tongue, plundered, and pulled back. Her urgent capable hands caressed Emie's upper arms, her back, her thighs. Emie's tongue made a tentative approach, and Gia sucked it gently into her mouth. Emie gasped.

Their eyes met. Held.

Time stopped. Breathing ceased.

Then another wave of passion rolled over them.

Emie never imagined a simple kiss would be this good, this right. Gia felt so soft and warm, so brazenly female, Emie couldn't get enough. She yanked impatiently at Gia's T-shirt, pulling the tucked front of it from her waistband. Emie's palms sought the bare, unbearably smooth skin she'd admired from afar for what seemed like forever. When she caressed her hands over Gia's toned, rippled stomach and flicked the pads of her thumbs over Gia's distended nipples, Gia simultaneously sagged and groaned, melting against Emie. Emie explored further, digging her fingers into the width and curve of Gia's lats.

Gia eased her farther back until her head met the mirror—a little harder than planned. Emie's hand went to her head. She chuckled.

"I'm sorry." Gia laughed too, but Emie quickly swallowed the sound with her ravenous mouth, and Gia made zero complaints.

Overcome with the need to rock her hips, Emie clambered closer, none too gracefully, and knocked a hairbrush off the vanity. It clattered on the tile, followed quickly by the soap bar and toothbrush holder. She didn't care. Gia didn't seem to, either. She pressed the epicenter of her throb into Gia's stomach, near the exploding point. Those long artist's fingers found their way to her breasts. Gia cupped and lifted her, deftly undoing the front clasp of her bra and pushing it away from her flesh. Emie arched her bare breasts into Gia's palms and hung her head back to allow Gia's hot lips access to her neck.

The doorbell rang.

Who cares? Go away. Busy. No one home.

It rang again.

Emie's eyes flew open. Oh no, Iris. Iris, who had been instructed to convince Gia that Emie's Mistress of the Dark look was unacceptable. But Gia obviously liked the way she looked, and Emie definitely approved of the way Gia felt.

Shit. Shit. Shit!

Change of plans.

She had to get to Iris before Iris got to Gia.

"Stop. G, stop! Wait!" Gripping Gia's shoulders, she pushed her back and managed to knock a few more toiletries to the floor.

Gia looked stunned, distracted. "But I—"

"I h-have to—"

"Wait, Em. I—" she whispered, in a husky tone.

Gia leaned toward her again, but Emie gripped her shoulders to stop her. She was panicked, thinking Iris might use her spare key and inadvertently ruin things just when they'd started to get good. "No…I can't. Just let me get off the—"

She half fell off the vanity, straightened her clothing, grappled for her bearings and her bra clasp simultaneously. Feeling lust-drunk and crazed for Gia, she smeared at her mouth with the back of her hand. She couldn't find words to explain. "It's Iris." Her gaze dropped for fear Gia would see the truth in her eyes. *How pathetic am I? I'd do my face this awful way just to have you want me.* "I have to…go."

Emie brushed past her, out the door, down the hall.

❖

Just like that, she was gone.

The stillness sucked Gia in like a vacuum. Blood raced in her veins. Her brain buzzed with painfully acute desire. With shaky hands, she stooped to pick up the items scattered over the bathroom floor, willing her uncooperative body to return to its normal state. She situated the toothbrush holder on the vanity, aligned the hairbrush neatly next to the basin.

Hard as she tried to ignore it, a sense of spiraling disaster swept through her. Remorse. She closed her eyes and rested her forehead on the front of the vanity. God, she shouldn't have kissed Emie. Hell, she'd practically ripped her clothes off and devoured her, and she knew how little experience Emie had in that arena, how little she *wanted* that experience. Whatever happened to Gia's gentleness plan? To taking her sweet time? She'd clearly pushed too hard, too soon. The panic in Emie's eyes as she'd escaped from the bathroom said it all.

You screwed up, G. She wanted your friendship.

You took advantage of that.

Gia stood and braced her hands on the countertop. She hung her head, letting her hair fall like a screen around her face. "Damnit." She'd wanted Emie to know she'd take her any way she could get her. Neighbor. Friend. Lover.

Lover. Desire surged.

No, that wasn't going to happen. "Damnit," Gia bit out again, raking the hair roughly back from her face. She straightened and stared at her reflection in the mirror with revulsion. Pushing people around to get what she wanted. Still. After all these years of telling herself she'd changed. Grown. Who the hell did she think she was kidding?

She'd fix this if she had to apologize, grovel, beg. She'd convince Emie it shouldn't have happened and assure her it would never happen again. She'd make it up to her, whatever it took. She would. Absolutely.

No matter what.

❖

Emie fumbled with the deadbolt and yanked the door open. "Come in," she barked. "Hurry up."

"What a lovely greeting," Iris quipped. Her features morphed from amused to mortified with one glance at the makeover results. "Lord have mercy, girl, you look like Night of the Living Dead." She crossed herself hastily.

"It's horrific, I know. But I don't care."

"Huh?"

"Shh. Just come on." Emie grabbed Iris's forearm and dragged her into the house. They stumbled through the living room toward the guest bathroom off the hallway. She shoved Iris in, slammed and locked the door behind them, then pressed her back against it. "Jesus," she exhaled, closing her eyes. Her hands curled into fists. "I can't believe that just happened."

"Quit freaking out and let me look," Iris said, her mind obviously on a different track. She grabbed Emie and centered her in front of the mirror, then stood behind her staring over Emie's shiny spikes at their reflection. Iris chewed the inside of her cheek, a disturbed wrinkle marring the perfection of her forehead. "Okay, first off, the lipstick should be *on* the lips, not spread around them."

"I don't care about the damn makeup," Emie rasped, peering guiltily at her confused friend while smearing the black from around her mouth with a tissue. She glanced in the mirror again. Holy hell. It looked like she'd been cleaning out the fireplace with her lips. So much for kiss-proof. "I knew they couldn't prove that scientifically," she muttered.

"Scientif—what?" Iris asked.

"Nothing. Never mind." Emie whirled, steadying herself with her palms on the sink edge. "Listen. New plan. You have to tell Gia you love it. That it looks great. I don't want her to know how much I hate it."

Iris's jaw dropped and her green eyes rounded with shock. "Girl, have you lost your mind? You can't go to your office party looking like this. You have more dignity than that."

"I know, but—"

"No, you obviously don't know." Iris gripped Emie's chin turned her face toward the mirror. "Look at it, for God's sake. I thought you told me Gia was a professional. What in the hell happened?"

"She *is* a professional." Emie batted away Iris's hand and gnawed her lip before deciding against it. She didn't want black teeth as well. She slumped onto the toilet lid, toes and knees pointing inward. Elbows on her knees, chin in her palms, she said, "I don't know what happened. I can't explain it."

"Try."

Emie inhaled. "All I can tell you is…Gia and I have managed to become friends."

"Yeah, Paloma told me that part. What's that got to do—"

"Just listen. Everything was working out fine between us. Then she made me up to look like this"—she framed her face with her hands—"and all hell broke loose."

"Hell?"

"Well, good hell."

Iris clicked her tongue and frowned at Emie. "Don't let your mama hear you say *that*, either."

Emie ignored her. "Iris, listen. Gia kissed me. *Really* kissed me. Like, Jesus, like I have never been kissed in my whole…" She choked up and shook her head, unable to finish.

Iris pulled her chin back in shock. "And that's hell?"

"Good hell, remember?" Emie swallowed, sensual excitement ribboning through her as she remembered just *how* good.

Iris busted into a Colgate grin. "But she kissed you?"

"Hoo-boy, did she ever." A feeling of wild passion reeled back and slapped her, and it took her a moment to gather her wits enough to go on. When she could speak again, Emie reached up and clutched her T-shirt at the neck. "She kissed me," Emie said again, "just before you got here. Hence the raccoon mouth."

"Em, that's so great. But I don't quite understand why you're looking so glum."

"It's complicated, I don't know."

"Is it that I interrupted? Could it have turned into more than a kiss?"

"Yes, but—"

Iris gripped her wrists and shook them, grinning. "Told you she had the hots for you."

"You don't understand. She has the hots for *this* me. And this isn't the real me." Emie's words sounded morose to her own ears, as well they should. "Gia has the hots for fucking Vampira, not for Emie Jaramillo. What am I going to do?"

Iris slid down the wall and sat cross-legged on the floor. "Em"—she uttered a sound of disbelief—"don't be an idiot. Gia can't possibly want you to look like that."

"Uh, are you forgetting she created this look? She told me I looked great. She doesn't even know I've seen it yet. Besides"— Emie spread her arms wide and spoke in a sarcastic tone—"did she ever kiss me in my natural state? No. She acted more like my sister until today."

"Did you encourage her to kiss you before? No," Iris countered, mimicking Emie's snideness. "Just the opposite. You told that walking sex goddess you wanted to be friends."

"Because she came here out of guilt, and nothing more. Don't you get it?" Emie rasped, scooting to the edge of the toilet lid. She pressed her lips together and struggled to lower her voice. "What am I supposed to do, Iris? Be grateful for the charity? You know that's not how I live my life."

"You're not"—Iris growled in frustration—"Emie, wake up. God, you can be so irritating. Tell Gia you don't like the makeover. Tell her you like a more natural look. Tell her you want her bod. Then get naked. End of story. Happily ever after."

Unbidden, tears rose to Emie's eyes. Her chin quivered, and a sob escaped. "It's so easy for you to say that, Iris. You don't get it. You're not me. You're gorgeous. Effortlessly gorgeous. I've never cared about that. I've devoted my life to science, to my career. And I love it. I do. But seriously, freaking philosophy professors don't give me a second glance. No one does. They never have and I've never cared. Until now. I'm so confused."

"You've actively given off that standoffish vibe, Em. You chose that route, and you can change it anytime you want."

Emie sniffed, then yanked a tissue out of the box on the toilet tank. "And you honestly think a woman like Gia Mendez would be interested in me? Forgive me if I don't share your confidence."

Iris softened. "Aw, honey, why don't you just ask—"

"No. I can't. No way."

"Okay, okay, calm down."

"Gia probably has Frankenstein Syndrome," Emie said, her voice croaking. "A twisted lust for her creepy creation."

Iris unfolded her long limbs until she could kneel. She scuffled across the floor on her knees and wrapped Emie in a hug. "I didn't mean to sound flippant, Em. But you aren't giving yourself enough credit with this woman."

"I don't know how." Her entire body trembled. She was scared of losing something that wasn't even really hers. "I've never felt this way. All I know is, if she likes me this way, why would I want to change back to the way I looked before? To be the object of ridicule on national TV? And then again, I don't want to be the kind of woman whose sole focus is on her looks."

"If Gia truly cared about you, she wouldn't want to change you." Iris rubbed her back.

"Well, she did change me, so thanks a lot," Emie said, wryly.

"No, I meant—"

"Forget it. I know what you're saying. But some of us don't have women falling at our feet. I never even wanted women falling at my feet."

"You could have that, though. It's a choice."

"Right," Emie said, in a sarcastic tone. Pulling out of Iris's embrace, she tipped her head back, then pressed tissue-wrapped fingers beneath her lower lashes, not wanting to completely ruin the makeup job since she had to face Gia again. She sniffed and wiped her nose.

Iris laid her palm on Emie's cheek and smiled. "Honey, just tell me what you want me to do. I'm on your side."

"Let me deal with it," Emie implored her friend. "Tell her it looks good and be convincing. Okay?"

Iris sighed, chewed on the advice. "Em, if you really want me to, I'll tell her you're the bomb," she said, sounding dubious. "But this isn't *you*."

"I know, believe me. But I think I'm falling in love with her."

"Duh."

"Well, I've never been in love. And I don't know how else to handle it," Emie whispered, ignoring Iris's interjection. "Promise you'll just go with the flow? And don't think badly of me."

Iris smacked her in the arm. "Who do you think you're talking to here? I'm your best friend. Now, stop crying or you'll look like *Rainy* Night of the Living Dead."

Emie blurted a watery chuckle, then stood and leaned in toward the mirror. She managed to erase most of the smeared lipstick from around her mouth, then slapped her cheeks a few times trying to remove evidence of her tears. "Ahhhh," she intoned, releasing her tension. "Thank you for this, Iris. I ordered you Kung Pao Chicken," she said, her voice tremulous.

"Oh…good. Thanks. I'm starving," Iris said dispassionately. She looked completely worried and out of sorts.

Emie blew out a breath, stretching her neck from side to side. After shaking her hands out like a boxer prepping to enter the ring, she asked, "Are you ready?"

"Me? Are *you* ready?"

Emie's teeth sank into her black bottom lip as she worried a soppy tissue through her fingers. "No. But I'm not getting any readier. Come on." She unlocked the door, and with Iris at her heels, skulked down the hallway like a thief.

"Shoot, let me grab my purse." Iris turned back.

Emie spared her a fleeting glance but continued toward the living room. She thought about Gia, and her stomach twanged.

That kiss. Jesus, that *kiss*. It mostly involved their lips, sure, but it was soooo much more than a kiss. She'd felt it straight down to her soul. Definitely not your normal, everyday smooch. Gia had climbed right inside and become a part of her, until Emie hadn't known if it was her nerves or Gia's being stimulated to the shrieking point.

Oh, God. She wasn't *falling* in love with Gia.

She *was* in love with her.

And in lust. *That kiss...*

She wanted so much more.

Turning into the living room, she came face-to-face with Gia sitting awkwardly on the arm of the sofa. "Oh!" she exclaimed. Her hand fluttered up to her chest which flushed with heat at the mere sight of the woman. "Y-you scared me."

"I'm sorry. I—" Gia stood and crossed to her cautiously, looking peaked and intense. A few feet from her, Gia reached out, but stopped herself and pulled back. "Emie, listen. We have to talk about—"

"Hi, Gia," Iris interrupted. She paused in the doorway.

"Oh. Hi." Gia backed off and raked shaky fingers through the length of her still-loose hair, wary eyes moving from one friend to the other. When her boot heels hit the back of the couch, she sat. "I forgot you were here."

"I'm here," Iris said, with fake cheerfulness. She poked her thumb in the direction of the hallway. "We couldn't wait. We looked at her makeover in the downstairs bathroom. Sorry."

A very pregnant pause ensued.

No one moved.

Inhaled air kept filling Emie's lungs until she thought she'd explode and float around the room like confetti.

"And?" Gia's throat tightened on a swallow. "What do you think of it?"

"I love it," Emie blurted, the air whooshing out.

"She…loves it." Iris punctuated the unnecessary statement with a flash of nervous laughter.

Emie shot a staccato glance at Iris, then turned to Gia and forced a brittle smile. She wrapped her arms over her torso and didn't speak for fear she'd hiccup. Or cry. Or die.

Gia's jaw went slack. She blinked several times. Her face angled toward Emie. "You…love it? Really?"

Emie's head jerked up and down in a somewhat nod-like manner.

"But…the makeup? The hair? All of it?"

"Yes," she said. "It's exactly what I wanted. Thank you so much."

"Well…great." Gia bestowed a flat-lipped smile but looked vaguely ill. "That's just…great. She loves it," she added, to Iris, flipping her hand and shrugging at the same time. "What about that, Iris?"

Iris leaned against the doorjamb and sighed. "Go figure."

How in the hell could she possibly have loved it? Gia thought, bereft. She'd never felt so lonely. She'd deliberately made up Emie to look ghoulish, so she would realize how ridiculous it was to think that makeup, or the lack thereof, made the woman. But the whole plan had backfired big-time. Now she'd have to send sweet Emie off to an important faculty function looking like a spectacle. Either that, or she'd have to confess her whole devious plot. After the blow of *The Stillman Show*, she didn't think Emie would forgive her for a second helping of steaming humiliation, no matter how good—albeit misguided—Gia's intentions had been. But that horrendous makeup job. *Shit.*

And she loved it.

"I absolutely love it."

Gia blinked a couple times. Her gaze moved to the chic young woman standing beside her in the carriage house, Mimi

Westmoreland. After the makeover debacle, Gia had thought about cancelling the appointment with the prominent gallery owner that morning, and now she wished she had. She could scarcely dredge up the enthusiasm to pay attention to one of the most important art dealers in Denver, a serious career mistake. "Pardon?"

Mimi's perfectly coiffed blond hair didn't move when she swivelled to smile at Gia with absolute debutante decorum. She gestured at the painting of Emie with a hand sporting so many gargantuan rings, Gia wondered how she held her wrist up. "I said I love it, Ms. Mendez. The portrait. It's exquisite. My husband will adore it as well, I'm certain."

"Well, the subject is exquisite," Gia told her, staring at the Emie she loved. Pure, gentle, genuine. *Not hers*. She couldn't forget, Emie still wanted Elizalde, unbelievable as that was. She should've remembered that last night. *Before* the kiss. Another speeding bullet of regret and sadness pierced her heart. Direct hit. Zero survivors. Rest in Peace.

"I don't believe I've ever seen a portrait where the subject wore glasses. At least not one rendered so beautifully."

"Thank you." Gia sniffed the air covertly, hoping she'd fumigated the carriage house well enough. It had gotten to where she hardly noticed the overpowering odor of the paints and oils, but she knew it distracted some visitors. Then again, this particular visitor was in the business.

Ms. Westmoreland tilted her head this way and that, shifting her weight from one three-inch lizard heel to the other. One arm resting against her torso, she cupped the opposite elbow and bent her wrist, gesturing with two fingers. "The composition is first class. But, you know, that's not it, either," she said. She gripped her chin and stepped backward, scrutinizing the painting with a narrowed gaze and pursed lips. "It's the emotion in the piece, the life. I don't know how you pulled that off."

In spite of her desolate mood, Gia's heart began to pound. Mimi really seemed to like it. Consigning with the Westmoreland

Gallery could set her on her feet. She wouldn't have to leave Denver. *Or Emie.* She'd start over, make it up to the woman with whom she'd somehow managed to fall in love.

Ms. Westmoreland peered over at her like she'd just figured out the mystery of the century. "I've got it. It's her look."

Gia swallowed and turned to the portrait. "Her look?"

"Absolutely, Ms. Mendez. And you can't beat it." She directed her attention back to the canvas as well. "That lovely woman has the undeniable look of love."

Emie padded listlessly into the kitchen and shoved the coffee carafe under the faucet. Her muscles ached and her eyes had burned too much to even consider putting in her contacts. But her glasses felt oddly comforting on her makeup-free face. She felt like herself, four-eyes and all.

She'd cried herself to sleep last night after Gia had pulled her aside and told her the kiss had been a mistake. Jesus, a *mistake.* She even *apologized.* Said she felt awful about it and it shouldn't have happened. Gia might as well have driven a knife into her heart.

Emie didn't want to go anywhere, especially not with Gia, when she was feeling so vulnerable. But they had to shop for her outfit today. The faculty get-together was tomorrow night. So she'd suck it up and suffer through the shopping, despite looking and feeling worse than she had since the three days after *The Stillman Show.* What did she have to lose? Gia didn't want her, and there she'd stood, ready and willing to relinquish her pride and wear freakish makeup just to keep the woman interested. What a fool. A weak, desperate fool. That was *so* not her. The whole thing was a fiasco. Her life was a fiasco. How had that happened?

God, she loved Gia.

A groan escaped from deep within her soul. Almost against

her will, she moved to the kitchen window to peer across the lawn at the carriage house. Dappled sunlight shone on the roof. The Japanese maple near the back swayed in the slight breeze. With the big north-facing window, what a perfect studio it could be for Gia. If only she lived with Emie, she could move all the living room furniture out and have ample space to create, to make magic. If only Gia loved her back, it could work.

If only. If only. If only.

Story of her life. Why had she never noticed until now?

Gia's door opened. Emie inhaled sharply and ducked down. Shoot, had Gia seen her? Her heart pounded with embarrassment. She rose slowly and moved off to the side of the window, peering cautiously around the wispy white curtain. Gia stepped out and—

Emie's extremities went completely numb. Gia stood in the doorway with a perfect magazine-page blonde. The woman wore a tight suit with a leather lapel and cuffs. She reeked of money. They smiled and laughed with one another, and Gia looked utterly beautiful, completely carefree. She wore a Mandarin-collared pearl-gray shirt untucked over charcoal slacks that flattered her toned curves. Her hair—the hair Emie had clutched with unabashed desire and need—hung loose, catching the sunlight and the breeze.

The woman leaned forward to say something and touched Gia's arm. Gia didn't look like she regretted *that*. Sharp, ugly talons of jealousy tore at Emie's middle. She white-knuckled the edge of the sink and wanted to hate them both for being perfect and confident and completely out of her league. But she couldn't. Because she loved Gia Mendez with every clonable fiber in her body. Emie scoffed. And she'd always been so proud of her intelligence. Ha.

Gia reached a hand out to the woman, and the blonde took it but then pulled Gia into an enthusiastic hug. As Gia's arms wrapped around the woman, Emie imagined her intoxicating scent wrapping around her, too. Of course Gia would want a woman like that. Logically, why not? Hot tears of anguish blurred the image she wished she'd never seen. She wouldn't have had she not been staring at the carriage house longing for a dream she'd never realize.

As if the day weren't bad enough, now this.

She knew one thing: she couldn't bear to face Gia now.

CHAPTER NINE

After changing into jeans and a polo shirt, Gia traversed the back lawn toward Emie's house. Sunshine heated her hair and kissed her skin. Her steps felt weightless, and she couldn't keep the grin from her face. The day had started out so unforgivably bad, but it had turned around in a big way. A sense of hope imbued her. She couldn't wait to tell Emie the great news and unveil the portrait she'd been working on for so long. Maybe she could convince Emie that Vitoria Elizalde was nothing more than a sharp-edged bitch who would only end up breaking her heart. She still couldn't quite make herself believe Emie wanted that player. So she'd confess her feelings and hope Emie'd give her a chance. They could start over.

Mimi Westmoreland not only consigned *Look of Love*, she also selected five other pieces from Gia's collection and intended to dedicate one complete room in the gallery to a gala opening. The wealthy gallery owner seemed even more excited than Gia was about their new partnership. Mimi had even hugged her! Yes, Mimi and her husband belonged to the kiss-kiss pretentious upper crust, but Gia could tolerate that for this much of a coup. In the art world, the Westmorelands were big time, and that's what really mattered.

Gia jumped in the air and pumped her fist. Yes!

Her entire body felt energized, alive. All of this was because of Emie. She inspired Gia in ways that were hard to express, made her accept the woman she'd become and forgive the angry young bully she'd once been. Gia no longer felt the need to beg forgiveness from all the people she'd hurt. She merely had to ask for clemency from herself.

She knew that now.

Because of Emie.

When she was around Emie, Gia felt like a good person. That had never happened before, not with anyone. God, she loved Emie Jaramillo. More than she ever thought she could love anyone. She'd just needed to love herself first.

A lump rose to Gia's throat and her stomach flopped. She wished her mother was alive to meet Emie. Mama would be so pleased, and Gia would give anything to finally do something to make her mama happy and proud. And Phillipe—her brother—had to meet Emie. Mr. Fuentes, too. They wouldn't believe that Gia had found such a wonderful woman.

She laughed and lifted her face to the sun. Without even realizing her power, Emie had taken the mismatched colors and bare canvas of Gia's life and nurtured her into a pièce de résistance.

Gia would have her. Somehow.

Even if she had to rein in her feelings, bide her time.

Even if she had to dress Emie to impress another woman.

Sobered slightly, Gia slowed her steps. She had to admit, things between them weren't perfect. They might be three steps forward instead of two back if Gia hadn't screwed up so royally last night, forced things. Her jaw clenched, but she consciously released the tension. *No time for doubt—think positive.* She hoped, after she'd apologized so profusely, that Emie'd had time to forgive her for the kiss. Okay, so she'd read Emie wrong on that one. But she'd been so responsive, so goddamned sexy—even with the horrific makeup job—Gia was sure, in the moment, that Emie wanted her just as much. Until she'd run. Hopefully, they could get past it. Go shopping. Joke around again. Life would be good.

A persistent sense of foreboding shadowed her thoughts, though. There was the small matter of preparing for the faculty get-together and explaining why she had tricked Emie and gone the ghoul route with her hair and makeup during the trial run. But…she'd figure that out as she went along. Emie couldn't hold it against her forever, could she? She was a reasonable, intelligent woman. She'd listen to Gia's motives before casting her aside.

Please let her listen.

Gia took all three porch steps at once and lifted her knuckles to rap on the door. Before she could knock, something caught her eye. She froze, fist in the air.

An envelope.

White. Sealed. Taped at an awkward angle on the glass.

And right in the middle, in Emie's neat drafter's printing, was her name. *Gia.*

Her heart didn't thud; it didn't race. Rather, it seemed to stop dead, and everything inside her went ice cold. Emie had left a note on the door, which could only mean she didn't want to see her. Not good. Was it an eviction notice? A Dear John letter? Hate mail?

Gia unfurled her fist and pulled the envelope off the glass. With shaking fingers, she ripped open the top. The unmistakable scent of lavender wafted from the stationery and socked her in the gut. It smelled like Emie. Something stiffer weighted the bottom of the envelope. Gia peered in and frowned—Emie's credit card? Baffled, she unfolded the note and read:

> *Dear Gia,*
>
> *I'm not feeling well today, must've been the extra-hot sesame beef. I'm not up to visitors and I certainly can't go shopping. Please, go without me. I've listed my sizes below. I've also enclosed my credit card so*

you don't incur any expenses on my behalf. I'm sorry.
Get whatever you think is best. It doesn't matter to me.
I trust you. I'll see you tomorrow. I hope you're still
willing to do the makeover.
    Emie.

Gia crumpled the letter in her fist and glanced up to Emie's shrouded bedroom window. Bad sesame beef? Yeah, right. Emie couldn't even bear to see her in person. She disgusted Emie.

Hell, I disgust myself.

Her eyes stung. A soul-deep ache started in her throat and radiated through her body. She hung her head, feeling beaten and desperate. She would beg, she would change, she would die… for this woman. Couldn't Emie feel that? Gia had never meant to hurt her. And yet, she had. Not once, but twice. Maybe this was her karmic destiny.

You hurt enough people in the past, G. Now it's your turn to hurt.

"Emie," she whispered in a ravaged tone, unwilling to buy that eye-for-an-eye explanation. God help her, she couldn't bear to lose Emie now.

❖

"Gia?"

Hearing her name, she turned from the Precious Memories window, where she'd been staring at—or rather through—the wedding display for the last however many minutes. She didn't even know how long. She blinked at the tall, willowy, indisputably stunning woman weaving toward her through the passing shoppers.

"I thought that was you," Iris said, tipping her shades down to peer over them.

"Oh. Hey, Iris." Even dressed down and wearing dark glasses and a baseball cap, she looked every inch the supermodel. Her attempt at looking incognito would've amused Gia if she didn't feel like her heart had been ripped from her chest with a meat hook. "What are you doing?"

"Just shopping." She angled her head to the side. "You?"

Gia's mouth opened, but nothing came out. The truth? She'd been scuffling through the mall like a listless vagrant for the past three hours, cursing the person who had written that crap about "it is better to have loved and lost, blah, blah." She'd looked at clothing for Emie but hadn't had the heart to buy anything yet. She knew she was a goner when she found herself standing in the Hallmark store reading every single card in the From Me to You line. One of them had even made her eyes blur with tears. What was she doing?

Losing her goddamned mind, that's what.

She lifted her arms halfheartedly, then let them drop. "I really screwed things up with her, Iris." The insufficiency of the words that finally tripped off her tongue frustrated her. Even so, a small bit of the weight on her shoulders lightened just for having verbalized the truth.

A quiet moment passed, with stroller moms and mall-rat teens passing them in a blur of chatter and packages. Iris twisted her lips to the side while she studied Gia's face. "Look, Gia," she said finally, "you're a really nice woman, but Emie is my best friend. My soul sister. I absolutely won't stand by to let anyone hurt her."

"Neither will I," Gia said, firmly.

Iris remained protective. Wary. Claws out. "What do you want from her?"

"What do I—?" Gia moved closer. "I'm in love with her," she rasped, clutching her hands into fists. "Sick in love with her." When Iris didn't speak, Gia huffed and added, "What do I want from her? Everything. All of her. Forever. I want to make her happy."

Iris crossed her arms and blew out an exhale. "That's what I thought. But, geez, woman, I was starting to wonder." She swung her arm over Gia's shoulder and steered her toward the food court. "I'll make you a deal. Buy me a cappuccino and biscotti and you can spill your troubles to me. Then I'll tell you all the ways you and Em are total idiots."

Fifteen minutes, two coffees, four biscotti, and a jumbled, incomplete explanation later, Iris raised one perfectly tweezed brow and planted her elbows on the table. "You have no idea how relieved I am to know you didn't really think that freakazoid makeup job looked great."

Gia grimaced. "It was awful, yeah?"

"Ghastly."

"That's what I was going for. At least I succeeded at one thing." Sighing, Gia ran a hand over the top of her head and let it rest at her nape. She stared at the best friend of the woman she loved. "But she wasn't supposed to like it, Iris. She was supposed to realize…something. I don't know. I can't even remember now and who cares anyway? It's over. She loved it. I can't believe how badly I screwed up. Fuck." She hung her head.

"Gia," Iris ordered in a droll tone. "Look at me."

Gia complied.

"Here's the thing you aren't getting." She knocked a knuckle on her temple. "Emie *didn't* like the makeup job, dummy."

Gia blinked. Twice. "But she said—?"

"Get real, sister." Iris spread her arms wide. "She hated it. She despised it. How could she not? I won't even tell you the words she used to describe it."

Shock zinged through Gia like metal balls in a pinball machine. Pandemonium broke loose in her brain.

Emie said—

Gia thought—

They made a deal to—

But what about—

Iris took advantage of Gia's moment of dumbfounded muteness to sip her cappuccino, eyeing her over the paper cup's rim.

"Then…why did she say she loved it?" Gia sputtered finally. "Love." She aimed a finger at Iris and narrowed her gaze. "I distinctly remember her using the word 'love.'"

Iris wiped her lips daintily and looked at her like she was a hopeless, hapless imbecile. "Because, news flash, dumbass. She *loves* you."

Her heart bungee-jumped. Could it be true? Even so, claiming she loved the horrid makeup job didn't make sense. "That doesn't explain why—"

Iris stopped her with a palm held high. "Em somehow got it implanted in her brain that you only became attracted to her when she transformed into Elvira on a heavy makeup day." She zigzagged her hands through the air at the ridiculous notion. "Something about a kiss."

Gia ground her teeth. "I knew I shouldn't have kissed her."

"Oh, no. You *should've* kissed her. Hell, you should've ripped her clothes off and made her scream Jesus. You just shouldn't have kissed her with her Monster Mash face on. That, my friend, was your crucial error."

Gia fixated on one part of her statement. "You're saying it was okay to kiss her?"

"Hell, yeah. Or it would've been, a couple weeks ago."

"But she said she only wanted to be friends," Gia said, in a lukewarm effort to defend her lack of action. "She told me she didn't want entanglements or something like that."

"Um, forgive my blunt response here, but, *duh!*" She widened her big green eyes. "Emie said that to maintain her dignity."

"Huh?"

"Swear to God, you are two of the most clueless women I've ever known. This is like a fucking science project." Iris sighed. "It's like this. Emie refuses to believe that a woman like you would be attracted to the real her. Which, of course, you inadvertently reinforced by kissing her while she was in full war paint last night."

Gia didn't even address the "woman like you" comment,

though it registered in her brain. "That's ridiculous. I've been telling Emie how amazing she is since the day I arrived in Colorado."

Iris gentled her tone and gave Gia a small, sympathetic smile. "Yes, but based on the way you two met, you can hardly blame her for doubting your motives."

Ouch. Gia pressed her lips together. The truth stung. Parts of Iris's explanation made sense, but a couple crucial puzzle pieces were missing. "There's one thing I don't get in this whole fiasco," she said.

"What might that be?"

"If she supposedly loves me, why does she want to impress that hag, Elizalde?"

Shock registered on Iris's face, then she hung her head back and laughed out loud. When she looked back at Gia, tears shone in her eyes. "Gia—God! You're so dense, you may as well be a man. You and Emie are a perfect match. You're both insane."

Gia tried for indignant, but only managed befuddled and forlorn. "What's that supposed to mean?"

She reached across the table and grabbed Gia's hand, her tone measured and distinct, as if she were speaking to a child. A not-too-smart child. "Emie doesn't *want* Elizalde, punkin. She wants that bitch to be attracted to her so she can turn her down flat. Humiliate Vitoria like the idiot did her. Get it?" She paused to let it sink in. "The whole *point* to this ridiculous makeover scheme is so Emie can seek revenge. I thought you knew that."

"What? No."

"Yeah. Incidentally, I've never approved of any of it."

Holy shit. It made sense. One corner of Gia's mouth, then the other, creaked up into a smile. Emie loved her.

She loves me.

They just had to find a way to bushwhack through the rainforest of their combined stupidity and everything would be fine. Right? Except Gia still had to make over Emie for the "event," and how exactly would she pull that off? Her smile dropped. Emie still planned to go through with this revenge scheme, and though Gia was vehemently opposed to the whole idea, the last thing in the world she wanted to do at this point was boss Emie around. She frowned. "How am I going to get out of this, Iris?"

She shook her head. "I've supplied the inside track, Gia, but you're going to have to dig yourself out on your own. If you truly love her, *focus* on her. Then you'll figure it out."

"But, do you think she'll"—she swallowed past a raw throat—"forgive me? For the makeup job? Everything?" Gia rested her forearms on the table and wound her hands into a tense ball.

Iris leaned forward and patted the knotted fists. "Last tip for ya, smartie. Lose the black lipstick." She stood and hiked her bag onto her shoulder. Donning the "I'm-not-who-you-think-I-am" sunglasses, she smiled. "Thanks for the java. Good luck."

By the time late Friday afternoon rolled around, Emie had resigned herself to facing Gia again. Eh, what the hell? She'd never really expected fireworks between them anyway. She just had to make it through the next hour…and the dreaded faculty get-together…then she could burrow back into her safe, predictable life and forget that this summer ever happened. As for Gia, Emie felt certain she'd quickly move on to bigger and blonder things.

So be it.

The teapot began to whistle. She whisked it from the heat and poured boiling water over a peppermint tea bag. Gripping the string, she dunked the bag absentmindedly in the mug. Her gaze strayed out the kitchen window toward the carriage house, willing Gia to appear so they could get on with it. Be done with it. To hell with it.

Sigh.

No sign of her. Big surprise. She'd long since learned that wishing for something didn't make it come true.

With a bone-deep bleakness, Emie carried her tea into the living room mainly to get away from the draw of that damned kitchen window. She curled up in the corner of the couch and picked up the latest issue of *Newsweek*, thumbing through it without interest. The blood-red orb of the setting sun dropped behind a stand of aspen trees, casting long, dark shadows through the window into the room. She didn't bother to turn on a lamp. She reveled in the darkness. In her next life, she hoped to come back as a bat. Or perhaps a mushroom. Anything that thrived in darkness.

Anything different from who she was this go-around.

Knock, knock, knock.

Gia.

Emie chucked the magazine aside and glanced toward the kitchen. Despite direct orders from her brain to the contrary, her throat tightened with anticipation. The really sick part was how much she wanted to see Gia. Still. She unwound from the couch, pulled her bathrobe tighter around her neck, and headed for the back door. Opening it, she looked directly into Gia's gorgeous honeyed eyes, then dropped her gaze. "Hi."

"Hey." A long uncomfortable pause ensued. "How are you feeling, *querida*?"

Feeling? she thought, glancing back up. The reddish light from the sunset burnished Gia's smooth bronze skin and cast a fiery luster to her long hair. The diamond in her earlobe reflected it, too, like a ruby.

Feeling? she thought again. What was that about? Ah, yes. Bad sesame beef.

"Better," she lied, clearing her throat. "Thanks for asking." She stood aside and motioned Gia in. As Gia crossed the threshold, both of them careful not to touch, brush up against each other, make any contact whatsoever, she noted the garment bag Gia carried, along with another bulky shopping bag. Curiosity got the better of her. "What did you buy?"

"An outfit"—Gia lifted the garment bag, then lowered it and raised the other sack—"matching shoes, hose in case you wanted them, purse, accessories, and…some cosmetics." She set both packages on the table.

"Cosmetics?" Emie frowned, nudging her glasses up. "Don't you think we got enough the other day?"

"Don't worry. This is all my treat," Gia said, with a small, winsome smile. "You've really done me a favor giving me a break on the rent. I just wanted to say thank you."

Emie didn't have the gumption to argue. "You're welcome."

"Plus, I thought we'd try a slightly different look for tonight and…we needed a few extra things."

"Oh. That's fine." But if Gia'd bought her a tight suit with leather lapels and cuffs, she'd die. Or cut the damn thing to shreds. "Want some tea?"

"Got a beer?"

Emie grudgingly smiled as she walked to the fridge. "If you were in kindergarten, you'd get a failing grade for 'gives appropriate answer to a question.'" She lifted a bottle off the refrigerator shelf and handed it over.

"Well, I never was a stellar student." Gia twisted off the cap and pitched it into the trash. "And I'm not in a tea sort of mood tonight."

What sort of mood was she in? Emie wondered. And why? Against her will, the beautiful scent of Gia—soapy, sugary, womanly—entered her sensory plane and gripped her heart. The very heart Gia had stolen when Emie hadn't been guarding it well enough. Hot tears stung her eyes. She blinked them back and bit her lip.

In one fluid motion, Gia set the bottle on the table and swept her into a heartbreakingly gentle embrace. One hand spanned her back, the other cupped her head and tucked it against her chest.

Emie reached up and pulled her glasses off her face. They stood like that for a long time, silent, swaying, her arms stiffly at her sides, Gia's wound about her. She felt Gia press her cheek, then her lips to the top of her head.

"Sweet Emie," Gia whispered. "I know you're nervous about tonight. And I haven't made it any easier for you. You deserve so much more than that."

"I-I'm fine," she lied. Her arms slipped around Gia's small waist, and she let the tears run soundlessly down her face to soak Gia's shirt. Why did she have to be so nice? The jerk. Emie just wanted Gia to hold her forever. Was that too much to ask?

"I promise I'll make it perfect for tonight, yeah?" Her lips brushed Emie's hair once again. "I think you'll like how I make up your face this time much better."

"Last time was okay," she muttered, apathetically.

"I didn't think so."

"Y-you didn't?" *What about that kiss?* She blinked against Gia's chest. "I got the impression you liked it."

"It was okay. But"—she felt Gia shrug—"not you. This look will be you. I promise."

"Not too much me. I have to attract Elizalde, remember?"

"How could I forget?"

Emie sniffled once deeply, then pulled away and smeared at her cheeks. "I'm sorry for that. I always get weepy when"—*my heart is breaking*—"uh, when I'm not feeling well. I've already shampooed my hair." Emie spun, picked up her mug, and headed for the front of the house.

"Okay. Why don't you wet it and wrap it in a towel?" Gia scooped up the bags and the beer and followed her. "Are you going to wear your glasses tonight?"

Emie scoffed. "No."

"Because if your eyes are irritated—"

"They're not," she snapped, then softened her tone. "Gia. They're fine. I'll just go put in my contacts."

"May I hang the outfit in your room?"

"Yes, go ahead. Second door on the right upstairs. Is it leather?"

"It's a surprise."

"Great," she said, her tone bland. "There's a hook inside the closet door if you want to put it there."

"Then I'll meet you in the bathroom," Gia said, "and we'll get this under way. Okay?"

Lifting the bottom of her robe, Emie started up the staircase with listless, heavy steps. *Gee, I can hardly wait.*

The intimate scent in Emie's bedroom, though gentle and understated, consumed Gia from the moment she entered. Gia hung the garment bag on the closet door hook, then arranged the hose, shoes, purse, and accessories in a neat row on the end of Emie's four-poster bed. Though she should've minded her own business and left, she couldn't stop herself from looking around.

The room was big, with a slanted ceiling on one side. A thick red down comforter covered the bed, and multicolored pillows lay scattered against the headboard. A wood-burning fireplace dominated the wall opposite the foot of her bed, and a neat stack of quilts and fleece blankets flanked it.

Gia moved to the mantel and studied the framed photographs. Emie's parents, some other relatives, she supposed. Was one of the older women the aunt who'd inadvertently stolen Emie's belief in love with her unintentionally careless words? Gia moved on to a series of photographs of Iris, Emie, and Paloma over the years. *Tres amigas.* She wished she'd cultivated such a strong bond with someone over the years. No sense wishing, though. A smile lifted her lips, and she reached out to touch an image of Emie. So lovely. So sweet.

She walked to Emie's bedside and scanned the nightstand, not really snooping, just trying to absorb the woman through her most private retreat. Freshly dusted, the nightstand held an alarm clock, several different-shaped candles nestled together on a sterling silver tray, and a stack of books for nighttime reading. Gia tilted her head to the side to read the titles:

Everything You Ever Wanted to Know about Oil Painting.
The Big Book of Oil Painting.
The Artist and His Studio.
American Painters in the Age of Impressionism.

Her breath caught. What was this? Touched, she sat on the edge of the bed and thumbed through one of the books. Her chest constricted and burned. If she didn't know better, she'd think she was heading for some kind of attack. But no. It was love.

Just love.

Quiet. Safe. Consuming.

She shut the book and smoothed a palm over the cover. That Emie cared enough about her to immerse herself in Gia's life's passion was…so like Emie. She thought of everyone but herself. Gia thought of the Westmoreland Gallery and excitement bubbled inside her. She wanted so much to share the good news about the gallery showing, but she preferred to make things better between the two of them first. Tonight was all about Emie. So she would wait until the time was right—something she was slowly learning to do, being in Emie's life.

Smiling, she took one more look around the room. In it, through it, she really saw Emie, the woman. And she felt at peace with what she had planned. She wouldn't pressure, force, or cajole. She'd just lay her heart out there, bold and bare, and leave it up to Emie to decide.

Gia crossed to the closet and pulled one more item out of the shopping bag.

A single, perfect pink rose. No thorns.

She hadn't been sure about the gesture until now, thinking perhaps all the Hallmark cards she'd read had poisoned her brain and turned her sappy. But no. Gia wanted Emie to have it. Cradling the blossom in her palm, she carried it to the head of the bed and laid it there, where Emie was sure to find it. Then, she kissed her fingertips and touched them to the pillow as well.

Just for good measure.

❖

Déjà vu.

Before she knew it, Emie found herself perched on the sink with Gia standing in front of her completely focused on her face. She could barely enter this room without remembering, feeling, reliving that kiss. But in this position, with everything so perfectly replicated, Gia's sinewy strength and oh-so-familiar scent suffocating her senses, Emie found it utterly impossible.

She could be a fool once, even twice, but three strikes, baby, and she was out. Forcing her mind from how Gia had felt and tasted, Emie reminded herself what she'd seen from the kitchen window. She reached up and touched her styled hair, stunned to find it soft.

"Better than the spikes, yeah?" Gia asked, almost shyly.

Emie's heart lifted, but she refused to hope. She lowered her chin. "You're the expert."

"You're going to like this, *querida.*" Gia's cheek dimpled with the smile, and she nudged Emie's lightly with her knuckle. "You look beautiful already, and we're not even done."

"Don't get carried away."

"I'm not, Em."

"Whatever you say," she said, dubiously. Still, the reassurance wrapped around her like an embrace she so desperately needed. She'd never been focused on her looks. But for tonight, just this once, she hoped to look stunning. Just the visual "screw you" Vitoria so richly deserved. Still, Emie tried to ignore the intimacy she felt between Gia and herself. After all, Gia had been affectionate once before as she made her up to look like someone she wasn't. Emie wouldn't fall for it again. She glanced toward the new cache of overpriced cosmetics and noticed Gia had bought that beautiful paler shade of blusher she'd admired at the department store. Upon further inspection, she noted most of the colors were softer, more subtle. Hope swelled inside her, despite her newly bricked and mortared emotional wall. Had Gia finally caught on to Emie's true desires? Had exotic gone the way of VHS tapes? She hoped so, because what she really wanted was elegant, not exotic. She just hadn't known how to express it before.

"I want to tell you something, Em, but I have to get it all out before you interrupt." Gia pulled a fluffy mascara wand from the tube and held it up. "Okay?"

The words brought Emie's gaze to Gia's pensive face. "Okay."

Gia moved her finger from Emie's eye level to the hollow of her own neck. "Stare here and don't blink." She waited until Emie did so, then began slowly stroking mascara on her lashes. "What Vitoria Elizalde put you through was despicable. But my part in the whole fiasco…and the aftermath hasn't been much better."

Emie's lips parted ready to stammer a denial, but Gia held up a hand, mascara tube clutched between her fingers.

Gia waited until Emie settled back. "I promised to be your friend, and I fell down on the job. Not intentionally, but because I became so blinded—" *a swallow* "—by my desire for you, by how you made me feel."

Emie's gaze lurched upward to Gia's eyes. Gia immediately cringed and reached for a swab. "Whoops—mascara dots."

"S-sorry," Emie stammered.

Gia waved away her apology. "Now—" She made the stare-at-my-throat gesture again. Emie complied, and Gia went to work on the other eye. "I've had my share of scores to settle in my time, and I don't begrudge your need for…tonight. Just as long as you know that Vitoria Elizalde doesn't deserve you. Never has. And we both know you don't love her."

A surprised monosyllabic laugh blurted from Emie's throat and she splayed her palm on her chest. "Whatever made you think I loved Vitoria Elizalde, of all godawful people?"

Gia tilted her head to the side. "Emie, please—"

"I'm sorry. I'll listen." She made a zip motion over her lips. "Go ahead."

Finished with the mascara, Gia pitched it into the shopping bag. She sucked in a deep breath and held it, seeming to struggle with what she wanted to say. Finally, she picked up the lip-liner— nude, thank goodness—and got to work on her mouth.

"Bottom line is, I saw something I wanted desperately and I went after it. I pushed you too hard, Emie. I know that now. I got it into my head that I knew what was best for you, and that all I had to do was convince you however I had to, whatever it took." A beat passed. Gia sighed. "I was wrong. And I'm sorry."

Emie bit her lip to keep from speaking.

"But the whole thing is your fault, really."

"What?"

A smile flashed on Gia's face, but her expression quickly sobered and intensified. "It's your fault, because every moment I spent around you, *querida*, you made me love you."

Emie's heated gaze dropped. Gia gently lifted her chin.

Their eyes met again, and held.

"But more importantly, every moment I spent around you… you made me love *me*." Gia implored Emie's eyes. "And that's something no one has been able to do for thirty-four long, lonely years." Gia's thumb brushed over Emie's bottom lip, sending shock waves straight to her spine. A winsome little smile curved Gia's mouth.

Tears rose to Emie's eyes.

"If you cry this makeup off, Emie, we're gonna have words."

"I'm sorry." She chuckle-sobbed and looked toward the ceiling until she'd staved off the tears as best she could.

"Now that my soul is bared and my chest is weight-free,

here's what I'm *not* going to do." Gia paused to coat a lip brush with soft plum color, then deftly filled in her lips. "I'm not going to tell you not to go through with tonight. I'm not even going to *ask* you not to do it. I support your decision, whatever you want."

She set the lipstick aside and placed her hands on Emie's shoulders. "I just want you to know that you have nothing to prove to Elizalde. Or anyone. Also, I'm not giving up, and I'm not going away. I'll be here for you, whenever, however you want me."

Before Emie could find the words to reply, Gia had slid her hands from Emie's shoulders to her wrists and pulled her gently from the vanity.

"Mira." Gia turned her around to face the mirror.

Emie's breath hitched. She didn't know if it was because of how lovely she looked or because Gia's gorgeous reflection shared the mirror with her in a way that just looked...perfect. Either way, the sight rendered her speechless. *This* was how she'd envisioned the makeover. *This* was what she wanted. Understated—she could barely tell she had makeup on—yet polished and elegant.

"See?" Gia said, voice husky. "You look like you."

"Only better," Emie added in a whisper.

Gia shook her head. "No, *mi corazón*, you look like *you*. Period. It doesn't get any better than that."

"Gia..." Emotion ached in Emie's throat. She met Gia's eyes in the reflection. "I love it."

"I love *you*," Gia told her simply, touching the tip of her nose. "Now, go get dressed. I'll wait for you on the back porch." Just like that, Gia turned and was gone.

Emie's heart buzzed with affection, with desire. However the wall still remained. Gia loved her, she claimed. *But, Gia,* Emie wanted to ask as the warmth in her soul began to cool, *what about the blonde?*

CHAPTER TEN

Emie retreated to her bedroom, mentally reciting every lyric she could dredge up about being a fool for love. Or *not* being a fool, that is. Yes, Gia Mendez was charming, sweet, kind, funny, gorgeous, sexy, persuasive—

Okay, this was getting her nowhere.

She'd fallen in love with the woman, but the point remained: though Gia had said all the right words and made her up beautifully, Emie had been hurt by her twice already in the short time they'd known each other. She couldn't afford to think with her heart right now if she didn't want to join the ranks of all the other damned fools who made ballad singers wealthy.

But was your pain really Gia's fault?

"Oh, shut up," she groused at her opinionated conscience. Squaring her shoulders, Emie marched to the closet and reached for the garment bag, then stopped herself. She was feeling flustered, not thinking straight. She might as well smooth lotion into her legs first since she'd decided to go without the constricting hose. Apprehension ratcheted up her spine at the prospect of the evening ahead and her woefully unplanned plan. She hoped to snatch her dignity back from Elizalde, but she really hadn't thought it through. Her mind had been…elsewhere. What in the hell was she going to do? She bit her lip, nervous tension dampening her palms. Everyone at the party would know about

The Stillman Show. They'd undoubtedly watch the interactions between her and Elizalde with bated breath. She hated to be the center of such negative attention. Damn Vitoria.

She didn't have to go, Gia had said.

Nothing to prove.

Not to Elizalde. Not to anyone.

Faltering, Emie wrapped her arms around her middle and studied her worried eyes in the mirror above her bureau. Yes, she *did* have to go. If for nothing else than to make a professional showing to her colleagues. It was the faculty mixer, for God's sake. It wasn't all about her. She might not have anything to prove to Elizalde, but she had a lot to prove to herself.

Emie Jaramillo might not be all that and a bag of chips, but she didn't retreat from a battle with her tail between her legs. She didn't hang her head in the face of humiliation. She didn't base her self-image on the opinion of one arrogant bitch.

But wasn't that exactly what she was doing?

Doubt whispered through her. She pushed it aside. "That's not the point," she said to her reflection. "Vitoria Elizalde deserves…"

What?

She wasn't sure and didn't care to ponder it. *Enough of this.* She needed to get dressed.

Emie turned to the bed and smiled, despite herself, at how neatly Gia had laid everything out. A little zing of surprise fired through her when she realized Gia hadn't gone for the thigh-high streetwalker boots like Emie had feared. Relieved, she eagerly examined Gia's selections. The dove gray suede pumps weren't too high, nor were they dowdy. They were sleek, fashionable stilettos that would do her smooth legs justice. Little gray pearl earrings and a necklace lay nestled next to a matching suede clutch purse. Lovely. Elegant. Just what she wanted. She had to admit, Gia was a thoughtful and perceptive woman.

Not to mention charming, sweet, kind, funny, gorgeous, sexy, persuasive—

"Stop it!" Emie whispered at herself. She was acting like a ridiculous, inexperienced schoolgirl who would titter and swoon at the attentions of the hottest girl in school. How could Gia claim to love her, anyway, when she'd only known Emie for a short time? Then again, Emie'd known Gia for the same amount of time, and she knew without a doubt she loved her…

But who was the blonde?

If only she hadn't seen. If only she *knew*. She should just ask Gia— *Damnit! Get it over with.* They weren't even twentysomething, they were thirtysomething. *This shouldn't be so freaking difficult.* But wouldn't Gia tell Emie herself if the blonde was nobody? Didn't she deserve that much from a woman who claimed to love her?

Maybe the blonde was…maybe she was a…cleaning lady.

Emie barked out a laugh. Yeah, right. The woman looked like she would vehemently deny the word "clean" could ever be used as a verb. No way was she a maid.

Forget it. Gia didn't owe her any explanations. She'd said she loved Emie—why should Emie doubt that? Why? Because… because…oh, hell. She just did. Why *would* Gia love her? was the real question. She didn't want to get hurt. Not by anyone, but most especially not by Gia. Was it so inconceivable that she'd want to protect her heart?

Frustration at herself surged. *That's it.* The wheels of fate had been set in motion. She was going to the party. Period. "Just get on with it," she muttered. Time was running out. She glanced at the luminescent green numbers on her alarm clock…and that's when she saw the rose. Gia had left a rose on her pillow.

The gesture struck her as so utterly sweet, it actually hurt. Waves of pain washed through her, over her, drowning her. She crossed slowly to the head of her bed and sat. Picked up the flower. Sniffed it. Gia knew how nerve-wracked she felt about the party tonight, and instead of begging her not to go or scoffing at her reasons, Gia had chosen to support her gently.

With a single rose. No thorns.

If only life were so kind.

"Don't even think about it," Emie warned the burgeoning tears threatening to streak her mascara. She wasn't going to ruin this makeup job. She stood, realizing with wry amusement that she'd been embroiled in a conversation with herself for the past several minutes. Didn't they give people complimentary white jackets and nice padded rooms for such behavior? Chuckling, she carried the rose into the bathroom and placed it in a cup full of water. After standing back to look at it, she decided to take it back into her room and set it on her nightstand so she could smell it later while she drifted off to sleep.

Another glance at the clock revved her engines. She needed to just *go*, before she became a shortsighted fool again. *Three strikes, you're out*, she reminded herself.

She double-checked her legs to make sure she didn't need the hose, turning her ankles side to side, finding them satisfactory, then crossed to the garment bag and unzipped it from top to bottom.

A small, reverent gasp escaped her lips. Inside she found the plum-colored silk and satin cocktail dress she'd admired the day they went cosmetics shopping. God. Gia really paid attention to her, didn't she? The gesture, like everything else Gia had done that day, reached in and lifted her emotions no matter how she struggled to hold them back.

She carefully pulled the gorgeous dress from the hanger and slipped it on. Perfect fit, and she adored it. The fabric swished around her legs and stopped just above knees that, really, didn't look so knobby after all.

Feeling slightly wobbly, a little teary, and dangerously close to shucking her pride and throwing herself into Gia's arms, she turned from the mirror. With shaky hands, she slipped on the jewelry and pumps, filled the little clutch with a few essentials, and hastened from the room. In the doorway, she hesitated. The mirror beckoned one last time.

Mirror, mirror, on the wall, who's the fairest of them all?

The answer to that question had never been Emie Jaramillo. And she'd never really cared, because her focus had been elsewhere. Then Vitoria came into the picture and scrambled up everything she'd known, the tenets upon which she'd built her life. Now, looking at herself in the elegant cocktail dress, with understated makeup and love in her eyes, *Emie felt beautiful, brilliant, and powerful.* For the first time. Thanks to Gia.

And yet, there was still the little matter of her dignity.

She needed to start the new semester on solid footing.

She knew Gia expected her to say good-bye, but that would be her undoing. Before she allowed her emotions to choose otherwise, Emie switched off her lamp, crept down the stairs, and slipped out the front door without speaking to Gia. She was going to the mixer. She had to. She didn't expect Gia to understand.

Emie had been at the party for an hour and had yet to cross paths with Elizalde. Dimmed crystal chandeliers lit the posh hotel ballroom, and well-dressed professors and other university staff members milled about laughing and enjoying the open bar and generous buffet. Scents of Italian oregano, marinara, grilled asparagus, and succulent roast beef mingled in the air. The festive atmosphere cheered her. Her angst over the evening dissipated with every passing minute.

Lifting her glass, Emie sipped the last of her wine, then set the goblet on the empty tray of a passing waiter. She'd spoken with many of her colleagues, and though several had said "Lovely dress" or "When did you start wearing contacts?" Emie never got the impression they were thinking, "And to think you were on that bookworm makeover show," as they paid the compliments. Of course not. The notion was ludicrous to her the more she thought about it. She was a well-respected, tenured faculty member and a renowned scientist at thirty, for God's sake. Most of the people in her circle were well-educated professionals who respected her for her mind and her contributions to the university. Just because Elizalde had tricked her onto the show didn't mean that the rest of her contemporaries gave a rat's ass about the superficialities of appearance.

She knew that.

She knew.

It hit her like a blow to the solar plexus.

When had her perspective gotten so skewed? Shaking her head, Emie picked up her clutch and went in search of the powder room.

Vernon Schell, a colleague up the chain on the research team, caught her arm as she wound through the tables. "Emie," his voice boomed as he pulled her into one of his famed bear hugs. "I was wondering if you were here. So good to see you."

"You, too, Vernon." She smiled, noticing the dark sun spots showing through the thinning white hair barely covering his tanned scalp. The deeply etched smile lines around his eyes bespoke of a life filled with joy. "How was your summer?"

"Super! Spent my time fishing for blue marlin off the coast of Florida and catching up on my reading." He guffawed. They exchanged more banalities of reacquaintance for a few moments before Vernon's ruddy, jowled face sobered, and he lowered his tone. "I've been meaning to pull you aside and talk to you, Emie." He looked contrite and pressed his lips together. "I should've called sooner."

Uh-oh. Her blood chilled. She'd managed to evade any mention of *The Stillman Show*, but here it came. She braced herself to endure Vernon's sympathy, lifted her chin, and forced a pleasant smile on her face. "What is it?"

"The study you published in *JAMA* last spring, about cloning's role in infertility treatment? It's been nominated for an award. We're all so pleased."

The shock must've shown on her face, because Dr. Schell belly laughed and patted her shoulder.

"Don't look so surprised, Doctor. The research was flawless

and the article impeccably written. Logical enough to give even our staunchest detractors pause." He beamed, laying a thick freckled finger over his lips as he studied her. "Anyway, that was the good news, here's the bad. The university president would like you to travel to Washington shortly after the term starts to present the data to a congressional task force." He twisted his mouth to the side. "That ought to throw a monkey wrench into your class schedule, which is why I should've called sooner. My most sincere apologies."

She quickly gathered her scattered composure, then reached out and squeezed his hand. So much for her thinking the stupid *Barry Stillman Show* was foremost in everyone's mind. "Are you kidding, Vernon?" She splayed a hand on her chest. "Don't apologize. I'm thrilled."

Another rich guffaw shook Vernon's notable girth. "Isn't that just like you to adapt to whatever is thrown your way. I must tell you, Dr. Jaramillo"—he leaned in, his forehead crinkled as he peered over the half-spectacles that Emie always thought made him look like Santa Claus—"you're going to have to learn to be much more of a tantrum-throwing elitist if you want to leave your mark on the annals of self-important professordom." His eyes twinkled.

Emie tossed her head with laughter. The thing she'd always loved about Vernon was his absolute refusal to take himself or his position too seriously. If anyone had a "right" to be impressed with himself, it was esteemed professor Vernon Schell. And yet, he wasn't. She could take a lesson or two from him. "I'll work on that," she said, tongue-in-cheek.

"Please don't, Doctor," he implored, with a wistful sigh. "Would that there were more just like you…" Leaning forward, he patted her cheek, then made his way past her through the crowd.

Emie still felt warm and fuzzy from Vernon's genuine compliments as she pushed through the door of the multi-mirrored powder room. She was heading through the tastefully appointed sitting area toward the toilets when a captivating young woman caught her eye. She smiled at exactly the same moment as the other woman. Then she froze.

My God.

It was *her own reflection.*

She took a tentative step toward the glass, then the mirror behind her caught the facing mirror image and unfurled it to infinity. She'd always thought it bizarre and a little magical when confronted with such reflective tricks. But this time was different. Better.

Feeling as giddy as a child at a carnival, Emie stared at her reflection. She couldn't believe the woman she'd glimpsed—admired, even—was none other than herself. Odd that a simple perspective shift, seeing herself as a stranger for a split second, had clarified far more for her than all the time she'd spent bemoaning her unfortunate appearance on the stupid *Barry Stillman Show.* What a fool she'd been. She looked like herself. *She looked fine.*

Hadn't Gia told her that since the moment they'd met?

Emie didn't blink, didn't draw a breath, didn't move as the moment of clarity rocked her world. All along, Gia had been attracted to her. From the beginning. Emie was the one who'd put the brakes on any advances, and Emie was the one who'd run out of the bathroom after their mind-blowing kiss without so much as an explanation. Gia had obviously misinterpreted her panic to get to Iris as...something else. Revulsion? Regret? Hardly.

But how was Gia to have known?

Of course she had apologized—she was too much of a gentlewoman to break Emie's rules. *Just friends.* That's what Emie had demanded. She scoffed. Had she lost her mind?

And what exactly had she hoped to prove to herself through a confrontation with Vitoria Elizalde? Why would she try and regain her so called dignity by manipulating the reactions of a woman who didn't care about her instead of listening to a woman she loved? A woman who loved her?

Emie laughed and shook her head.

For an intelligent woman, she sure could be a fool.

Dazzled, Emie glanced behind her at the mirror, then back at the one before her. The repeating reflections looked like a hallway winding off into nowhere. Or perhaps a pathway to a rich, wonderful future.

She supposed it was all in one's perspective.

Why had she doubted Gia?

Why had she left her?

As though she'd never experienced a moment of confusion in her life, Emie realized what she had to do. Gia loved her. She absolutely had no doubt. There had to be an explanation for the blond-haired woman, because if Emie had learned one thing about Gia Mendez, it was that she was a woman of impeccable honor. Gia would never intentionally hurt Emie by pretending to love her while seeing another woman. Gia would never intentionally hurt her, period. She'd given Emie the freedom to do what she had to this evening, and now Emie would return the favor. She'd give Gia the opportunity to explain.

Gia loved her. That's what mattered.

She had to go to her.

Emie hurried from the powder room and—Murphy's Law—ran smack into none other than Vitoria Elizalde as she made her way toward the restroom. They both staggered back, and Vitoria's expression flashed with surprise and even…fear? The thought pulled laughter from deep inside Emie. Big, bad Dr. Vitoria Elizalde was afraid of her. What did the bitch think she was going to do? Drive a stake through her heart?

Hell hath no fury…

Emie squared her shoulders and gave a genuine smile. Actually, she ought to kiss the reptilian hag and thank her profusely. If not for Vitoria's stupid little ploy with *The Stillman Show*, Emie never would've met Gia. She wished the egotistical woman knew she was merely a pawn in the larger plans of fate.

"Hello, Vitoria," she said, enjoying the other woman's discomfort. "It's nice to see you."

Vitoria patted her already slicked-back hair. "It's nice to—? But of course. Dr. Jaramillo. You, too." Her gaze made a furtive dip to the exit and back.

Emie figured she was probably estimating her chances of escaping the pointy edge of that stake. She pictured herself as Buffy, executing a perfect roundhouse kick before shoving that stake in. Poof! Dust. The image amused her so much, she couldn't keep from prolonging the conversation. Just a little. "I assume you heard our infertility study is getting some notice?"

Vitoria swallowed slowly, seeming to try to gauge Emie's tactics. "Why isn't she pummeling me with her fists?" the Brazilian probably thought. What she said was, "Yes. Wonderful news. I am thinking the publicity will bring us additional grant monies. You should be...very proud."

"I am, thank you." Emie smiled, feeling powerful and giddy with hope. Enough of this. She felt like the all-powerful cat batting around the pathetic mouse before devouring it. Only difference was, she no longer had a taste for blood. "Well, I have to be going. See you in a week or so." She skirted around Vitoria, but the other woman's talon-tipped hand snaked out to stop her.

"Emie."

She turned and raised a questioning brow.

"You...you look lovely."

"Oh, I know." She tossed her hair, truly believing the words for the first time since that damned television show. "I'm in love. Does amazing things for a woman, don't you think?" Before Vitoria could respond, Emie eased out of her grasp and headed toward the exit.

Toward home.

Toward Gia.

꽃

Bright moonlight streaked through the picture window, casting silvery-blue illumination across the floor of the carriage house. Gia had pulled a chair over to face the glass, lacking the motivation to do anything else. She hadn't even turned on a light. Stars speckled the inky sky, and she might have found the view inspiring if she didn't feel so bleak.

Why had Emie left without speaking to her? Gia had thought the new makeover, the surprise of the dress she'd so admired would have melted at least some of the ice around Emie's heart. She'd believed she could get through to Emie, but perhaps the tally of mistakes had just been too long to overcome. The thought that she'd missed her chance with the most amazing woman in the world was a physical pain.

Gia saw Emie round the side of the house, high heels dangling from her hand, and stunned relief flooded through her. Guarded relief. At least Emie had come back. Elizalde hadn't latched onto her vulnerabilities and taken her for a ride, something that had worried Gia since the moment she'd realized Emie had left without a good-bye.

Wearing an adorable determined look on her fine-featured face, Emie hurried across the backyard...toward the carriage house. Gia's breath hitched. Good sign? She hoped so. She stood, cheek to cheek with her own reflection in the glass, watching Emie's approach. When she neared the carriage house door, Gia traversed the dark cottage in long, hasty strides. Reminding herself to hold back, not to push, to let Emie take the lead, Gia braced one arm against the door frame. Head hung, she closed her eyes and waited for the knock.

Tap, tap.

Gentle. Just like Emie herself.

Gia didn't waste time playing games, but threw the door open to greet her—the woman she prayed could learn to love her, imperfections and all. But, as she stood there in bare feet, the breeze ruffling her short, sassy locks, Gia's heart tightened and stole her words.

The sight of her in the silk dress that had obviously been designed with her sensuous, curving body in mind nearly knocked

Gia flat. The shy tilt to Emie's face didn't help, but Gia managed to remain standing. Barely. She couldn't quite get a handle on Emie's expression. She didn't look angry, or apathetic, as she had during the makeover. Hope gleamed in her eyes. That, and… apprehension?

For God's sake, the two of them needed to stop tiptoeing around each other and just *talk.*

Gia furrowed nervous fingers through her hair and started simply. "You're back."

"Yes." Emie studied Gia's face for a moment, swinging the gray shoes hooked over her fingers, then inclined her head toward the dark room behind her. "Busy?"

"Never too busy for you."

Emie bestowed a small smile. "May I?"

"Of course. Just let me—" Gia left her standing on the threshold and navigated through the shadows to the lamp. With a snap, golden light flooded the small cottage, curling its way into the darkened corners. She turned, finding Emie's wide eyes moving around her living and working space with curiosity. Emie stood awkwardly in the doorway, looking as though she might bolt at any moment.

"Come in. Please." Gia waited until Emie had stepped tentatively forward before asking, "How did it go?" She felt as if they were circling each other in slow motion, neither quite sure of the other's motive or next move.

"It was…illuminating." Emie said, cryptically, punctuating the statement with a winsome smile. "Thank you for the dress."

"It's perfect on you," Gia said, but it was more of a whisper. The night air felt balmy, but goose bumps coated her flesh. Why did it seem like this moment was the culmination of every second of her life up till now? "You're so…God. Em, you're so beautiful in it."

Blush colored her cheeks. She looked down, then up at Gia again. "I didn't know you noticed it that day in the mall."

Gia swallowed and spoke slowly, afraid of screwing

everything up again. She couldn't quite maintain her bearings around Emie. "Everything that's important to you, *querida*, is important to me. Of course I noticed." A tight pause ensued, so Gia changed the subject. "You're home early."

Emie nodded. "I...wanted to be."

Gia reached out for her but stopped, curling her hand back and dropping it to her side. "What happened at the party?"

Emie trailed her finger along the small kitchenette table near the door and set her shoes on the chair. "Well, I found out I won an award," she said, lightly.

"An award?" Emie seemed almost playful. Gia decided to follow her lead. "Best dressed?"

"No."

"Prettiest girl?"

Emie chuckled and met her gaze, voice thick with emotion. "Nope, not that one either. A better one."

The heat Gia saw in Emie's eyes rocked her. But it was tempered with...something. Unable to stop herself, she crossed to Emie, stood close enough to notice an eyelash on her cheekbone. Gia brushed it off, smoothed her hand through Emie's hair, and cupped her cheek in one fluid motion. "Tell me." *Before being this close to you, this much in love with you, makes me unable to hear a word you say.*

To Gia's surprise, a ripple of worry darkened her eyes and she bit the corner of her mouth.

"What is it?"

"Sit with me." She pulled out one of the chairs and nestled into it with a sigh. "I'm not used to heels. My feet hurt."

Deep within Gia, fear crackled with electricity. There was something more, something bad. She could feel it like an impending storm. Had Emie come to say good-bye? Good riddance? They sat, didn't speak. Gia inhaled deeply. Finally, when she couldn't bear the suspense, she whispered, *"¿Qué pasó?"*

Emie sucked in a breath, held it, then whooshed it out. "I won an award for an article I wrote about a study I headed. Published in a professional journal." Her fingers reached out and wound with Gia's on the table. Squeezed. "The university is sending me to Washington in a few weeks to speak before some sort of congressional committee."

A rush of air left Gia as her heart swelled. She shook her head. "You're amazing, baby. I'm so happy for you."

"Thank you. It really is an honor."

But that really hadn't answered Gia's question. She wanted to know what was holding Emie back, what put the worry and fear in her doe eyes. Gia still felt it. Definitely something Emie wasn't saying. So help her, God, if Elizalde hurt Emie again. "Why did you leave the party early, *querida?*"

"Because I wanted to see you." Tears flooded Emie's eyes.

The inner alarm compounded. "What's wrong? Talk to me." Gia rose from her chair and crouched in front of Emie, gently caressing her legs from knee to hip. "Emie, please. Did Elizalde—?"

"No." Emie swiped a tear and sniffed. "It's not that."

Gia's jaw clenched. "I'll kill her if—"

"Honey," she said simply. "She's not worth it. I'm done with Vitoria and what she did to me. She's nobody. Besides, I sort of owe her a debt of gratitude."

Gia squinted. "Come again?"

"If she hadn't tricked me onto the show, I would never have met you."

Hope whirled through Gia. What did Emie mean? No assumptions. If she was happy fate brought them together, then— "What's troubling you?"

Emie bit her bottom lip hard enough that Gia winced just watching her.

"I-I have to ask you something, Gia. And…it's not going to sound so good. Stupid, even. But I have to. Please understand."

"Ask, *querida.*" She spread her arms and smiled, feeling so much love for this vulnerable yet powerful woman. "My life is an open book to you."

Emie tossed her head, looking off toward the stretched canvases and paintings leaning against the walls. "Yesterday, I was making coffee." She swallowed several times and wicked away more tears.

Gia waited. She couldn't help but notice Emie seemed embarrassed. Almost apologetic.

"A-and…I'm not a…suspicious person normally, but I-I've been so hurt. It's no excuse. I know that. God, I'm not sixteen. I have a PhD." She waved her hand weakly. "Anyway, I saw you." Her face crumpled. More tears. "Coming from your house. With…with a woman, and I just—"

Realization dawned, and Gia nearly laughed with relief. Emie thought she had another woman? As though Gia could ever look at anyone else but sweet, generous, brilliant Emie Jaramillo. But the best thing about this whole misunderstanding was—*Emie cared.* Gia felt it now, the solidity of it, the truth. "Oh, no no. Do you mean the hug?"

Emie nodded, looking weepy and sheepish.

Gia leaned closer and cradled Emie's face in her hands. "It's not what you think. Why didn't you bring it up sooner?"

She studied Gia's eyes, then shrugged. "Who was she?"

Gia had planned on waiting until the time was right to show her the painting, and the time couldn't get any more right than this. Instead of answering her question, Gia stood and reached out a hand. "Come. I'll show you."

Emie stared up at her, then rose unsteadily to her feet. Gia tucked Emie's arm into the crook of her elbow and pulled her closer. Together they walked toward the cloth-draped canvas on the easel. Gia leaned her head closer to Emie's. "You remember I told you I had caught the interest of some gallery owners who wanted to view my work, yeah?"

She nodded.

"The woman you saw was Mimi Westmoreland. She and her husband own one of the most prestigious galleries in Denver."

"Yes, I know of it." With a sharp intake of breath, Emie glanced up, wide-eyed. "And?"

Gia grinned, too proud and excited to rein in the emotions. "And they love me. My work, that is. They consigned several of my pieces and I'm going to have a private opening."

"Gia! But that's wonderful." Emie threw her arms around her neck and Gia lifted her, swung her around.

Laughing, she set Emie on her feet but didn't release her. Their bodies, from breasts to shins, pressed together, and the perfection of Emie's softness molded against her own body shook Gia's composure. She smoothed one palm down Emie's back, just to the curve of her sexy ass. Drinking her in with loving eyes, Gia whispered, "It's common practice for a gallery owner to visit the artist's studio to view her work. When you saw me, Ms. Westmoreland and I had just come to a very favorable business agreement." Gia took the chance and kissed the tip of Emie's nose. "That's all."

Emie groaned. "God, I'm an idiot! An insecure idiot. I'm so sorry I asked. Why didn't you tell me?"

"I came to tell you." Gia dipped her chin. "But I found an envelope taped to the door instead."

Emie's cheeks reddened. "I feel stupid. I should've known. I should've trusted you." She buried her face into the plush safety of Gia's chest.

"I never gave you much reason to." She kissed Emie's hair.

"You never gave me reason not to."

"It's over," Gia whispered. "*No te preocupes*. If I'd seen you hugging another woman, I would have gone mad and ripped her limb from limb."

Emie glanced up, eyes widened. "Really?"

"Not really. I'm not that kind of a woman"—she winked—"remember?"

"I do," Emie said, on a soft laugh.

"I would've worried, though."

Emie expelled a breath. "Thank you for saying that."

"Wait. There's more."

"More?"

Gia reached up and deftly pulled the air-light silk from the painting, then stepped back to allow Emie an unobstructed view. Her gaze moved from Emie's profile to the painting and back, heart pounding wildly. She wanted Emie to love the portrait as much as she did.

"My God," Emie breathed, mesmerized. She clutched her fists at chest level. After staring open-mouthed for several seconds, she licked her lips. "It's me."

"Yes."

Her eyes glistened with raw emotion. "I look…"

"Beautiful," Gia whispered, moving closer. "Just as I've always seen you. Just as the world will see you in the Westmoreland Gallery, *mi corazón*."

"Oh, Gia. I'm…speechless. Is this what you've been working on so diligently?"

"Yes. This is the piece that made Mimi Westmoreland hug me." Gia reached out and traced Emie's cheekbone. Her skin felt like silk, powder, rose petals. She was excruciatingly soft and pliant. "So, you see, once again, this whole thing is all your fault."

Emie laughed, inclining her head to stare at her bare feet. When she looked up again, her gaze sizzled. She reached out and touched Gia's lips. Gia's eyes fluttered closed as desire ripped through her. She wrapped her hands around Emie's wrist and peppered her palm with soft kisses.

"You're so gentle with me, G."

"You make me feel gentle, *querida*."

"Well, you make me feel perfect, just as I am. So we're even." Emie sighed. Gia opened her arms, and Emie melted willingly into the embrace, holding her tightly, kissing her chest through the T-shirt.

"Emie, you feel so right in my arms."

"Then let me stay here," she whispered.

"For as long as you want, baby. It's all I've wanted."

She pressed her cheek against Gia's heartbeat. "We've made some mistakes, Gia."

"That's okay." Gia smoothed Emie's soft hair with a palm. "We have time to correct them. All of them."

Emie's head came up. Her eyes searched Gia's face, looking more secure, more brazen. Infinitely sexy. "You remember the kiss?"

Gia snorted softly. Did she remember it? It consumed her every waking thought and most of her dreams. "Ah…yes."

"If you recall, we got interrupted…" Emie said, trailing off.

A burning arrow of desire pierced Gia's heart spiraling down to pool, hot and heavy, low in her body. "Yes, we did."

"Well…" Emie nestled closer. Trusting. Loving. She ran her finger from the hollow of Gia's throat, between her breasts, all the way down the front of her, then hooked it in her waistband. "That was a mistake. Don't you think?"

"An unfortunate mistake."

"An unfortunate mistake that I think we should correct," Emie whispered. "Right now." With a not-so-subtle movement against Gia's body, Emie made it abundantly clear what she wanted.

"Are you sure?" The words came out husky.

"I've never been more sure of anything in my life. Iris always says the true test of a silk cocktail dress is how beautifully it floats to the floor."

Gia bent down and swept Emie into her arms, smiling as she carried her to the bed. She deposited this woman she loved so much onto the comforter and came down gently on top of her, intending to make love to her all night long If Emie allowed It. Hell, all week long. She ran her tongue into the sweet warm valley between Emie's breasts, one of many valleys on her beautiful landscape that Gia planned to explore with her tongue, her hands, every part of her body.

A tentative kiss grew almost instantly more urgent, and soon Emie was pulling at the buttons on Gia's shirt, tugging at the zipper of her jeans.

Gia closed her hand gently over Emie's. "Slow down, love."

"Are you kidding? I've wanted you for so long, slowing down isn't an option."

Gia paused, huffed out a short laugh. "We're idiots. You know that?"

"Yeah. Isn't it great?"

They laughed, as garment by garment, their clothing dropped to the floor next to the bed. Before long, their naked bodies were pressed together, skin on heated skin, and then they did slow down. Their gazes tangled, so intimately. Gia wanted to soak it all in, not rush things. Then again, her body screamed otherwise.

"What are you waiting for?" Emie asked.

"I…don't know. I'm trying to make sure this is real."

Emie threaded her fingers into Gia's hair and leaned up to kiss her deeply. When they broke apart, panting, Emie said, "It's real. I am naked in your bed, for God's sake, woman. Don't make me wait much longer or I'm going to flip you over and take charge."

The very thought sent a thrill through Gia. Her body throbbed, and she moved against Emie, edging one leg between those firm, silky thighs, only to find her hot and oh so wet. "What do you want?"

"You. All of you. Touching me. Tasting me. Inside me. And then I'm going to repay the favor, big-time."

Gia groaned, raining kisses on Emie's neck, her chest, before finally taking one hardened nipple into her mouth, tugging and nibbling. With her other hand, she cupped the soft, firm perfection of Emie's other breast.

She felt Emie's whimper of pleasure rumble in her mouth, which only urged her on.

Emie's hips raised, pressed into Gia's thigh. Crazed with desire, Gia wound one arm around Emie's back and pulled her harder against her leg, moving with primal desire as she released one breast to lavish attention on the other.

Their breathing grew more urgent, their movements more intense. Emie's legs began to shake, and Gia kissed her way down that beautiful body until she captured Emie's moist heat with her mouth.

Emie gasped and pressed against Gia's tongue, urging her on, spreading her legs wider. Gia found Emie's sweet spot and sucked, reaching down to ease two fingers, then three, into her slick, tight center.

"Yes," Emie whispered. "Harder."

Gia willingly complied, pulling Emie toward her, making love to her like she'd dreamed of for so long. When Emie's body contracted around her fingers, Gia curled up the tips to tickle Emie's G-spot, and within moments, Emie arched her back as a gush of hot wetness tantalized Gia's tongue. God, Emie tasted like heaven and felt like home. Gia didn't want to stop. She continued pushing into Emie's sweet body, deeper…deeper, until Emie reached down and grabbed hold of her wrist, chuckling.

"Stop. I can't take it."

Gia stilled her movements but remained inside Emie, enjoying the feel of her quivering aftershocks. She smoothed the wetness from her cheeks on the inside of Emie's thighs, then kissed her way up until she captured Emie's mouth with her own. The kiss lingered, until Gia couldn't discern the sweet taste of Emie's mouth from the erotic taste of her body.

Eventually, their breathing slowed, and she gently slid her fingers from inside Emie, only to be met with a disappointed groan that made Gia grin. "There's more where that came from, Em. This is only the beginning."

Their gazes met, tangled, connected.

Emie's eyes moistened, and she sighed. "G?"

"Yes, baby girl?"

"We're not done here."

"Thank God for that," Gia said, yearning to be vulnerable with a woman for the first time in a very long time.

Emie gently rolled Gia on her back and stilled. As her hand moved down Gia's body, her words came out wobbly, passionate, so filled with a promise Gia had waited a lifetime to hear. "I love you, Gia. So very much. Do you know that?"

"I do know, *querida*," Gia whispered, lifting trembling lips toward Emie's again as she opened herself up for the woman she'd waited a lifetime to find. "I can see it in your eyes."

About the Author

Lea Santos has been concocting tall tales since she was a child, according to her mother. Usually these had to do with where she was, who she was with, and whether or not she'd finished her math homework (which she hadn't). When it came time to pick a career, Lea waffled, then dabbled in everything from guiding tours in Europe, to police work, to bookkeeping for an exotic bird and reptile company—probably not the best choice, since (1) she never did finish that math, and (2) the Komodo dragons freaked her out. (A lot.) She eventually decided to go with her strengths and continue spinning wild stories, except this time, she'd turn them into whole books and call it a career. She rarely lies anymore about where she's been or who she was with…

Books Available From Bold Strokes Books

Fierce Overture by Gun Brooke. Helena Forsythe is a hard-hitting CEO who gets what she wants by taking no prisoners when negotiating—until she meets a woman who convinces her that charm may be the way to win a battle, and a heart. (978-1-60282-156-9)

Trauma Alert by Radclyffe. Dr. Ali Torveau has no trouble saying no to romance until the day firefighter Beau Cross shows up in her ER and sets her carefully ordered world aflame. (978-1-60282-157-6)

Wolfsbane Winter by Jane Fletcher. Iron Wolf mercenary Deryn faces down demon magic and otherworldly foes with a smile, but she's defenseless when healer Alana wages war on her heart. (978-1-60282-158-3)

Little White Lie by Lea Santos. Emie Jaramillo knows relationships are for other people, and beautiful women like Gia Mendez don't belong anywhere near her boring world of academia—until Gia sets out to convince Emie she has not only brains, but beauty…and that she's the only woman Gia wants in her life. (978-1-60282-163-7)

Witch Wolf by Winter Pennington. In a world where vampires have charmed their way into modern society, where werewolves walk the streets with their beasts disguised by human skin, Investigator Kassandra Lyall has a secret of her own to protect. She's one of them. (978-1-60282-177-4)

Do Not Disturb by Carsen Taite. Ainsley Faraday, a high-powered executive, and rock music celebrity Greer Davis couldn't be less well suited for one another, and yet they soon discover passion has a way of designing its own future. (978-1-60282-153-8)

From This Moment On by PJ Trebelhorn. Devon Conway and Katherine Hunter both lost love and neither believes they will ever find it again—until the moment they meet and everything changes. (978-1-60282-154-5)

Vapor by Larkin Rose. When erotic romance writer Ashley Vaughn decides to take her research into the bedroom for a night of passion with Victoria Hadley, she discovers that fact is hotter than fiction. (978-1-60282-155-2)

Wind and Bones by Kristin Marra. Jill O'Hara, award-winning journalist, just wants to settle her deceased father's affairs and leave Prairie View, Montana, far, far behind—but an old girlfriend, a sexy sheriff, and a dangerous secret keep her down on the ranch. (978-1-60282-150-7)

Nightshade by Shea Godfrey. The story of a princess, betrothed as a political pawn, who falls for her intended husband's soldier sister, is a modern-day fairy tale to capture the heart. (978-1-60282-151-4)

Vieux Carré Voodoo by Greg Herren. Popular New Orleans detective Scotty Bradley just can't stay out of trouble—especially when an old flame turns up asking for help. (978-1-60282-152-1)

The Pleasure Set by Lisa Girolami. Laney DeGraff, a successful president of a family-owned bank on Rodeo Drive, finds her comfortable life taking a turn toward danger when Theresa Aguilar, a sleek, sexy lawyer, invites her to join an exclusive, secret group of powerful, alluring women. (978-1-60282-144-6)

A Perfect Match by Erin Dutton. The exciting world of pro golf forms the backdrop for a fast-paced, sexy romance. (978-1-60282-145-3)

Father Knows Best by Lynda Sandoval. High school juniors and best friends Lila Moreno, Meryl Morganstern, and Caressa Thibodoux plan to make the most of the summer before senior year. What they discover that amazing summer about girl power, growing up, and trusting friends and family more than prepares them to tackle that all-important senior year! (978-1-60282-147-7)

The Midnight Hunt by L. L. Raand. Medic Drake McKennan takes a chance and loses, and her life will never be the same—because when she wakes up after surviving a life-threatening illness, she is no longer human. (978-1-60282-140-8)

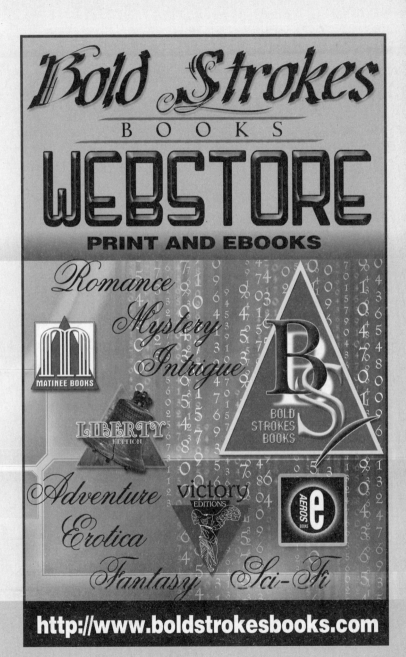